THE AFRICAN
REBELS

DR. FRANÇOIS ADJA ASSEMIEN

Library of Congress Control Number: 2024914593

ISBN
978-1-964488-17-2 (Paperback)
978-1-964488-18-9 (eBook)
978-1-964488-16-5 (Hardcover)

I dedicate this novel

To

His Excellency Mr. Barack OBAMA, President
of the United States of America

Sonia Sanchez (American writer)
Toni Morrison (American novelist)
David Bradley (American novelist)
Ishmael Reed (American novelist)
Al Young (American novelist)
JAMES Alan McPherson (American novelist)
Gloria Naylor (American novelist)
Clarence Major (American novelist)
JOHN A. Williams American novelist
Alice Walker (American novelist)
John Wideman (American novelist)
John Fireston family in Akron.

Table of Contents

CHAPTER 1

On behalf of Toissin, the African philosopher, I went to the appointment given to me by the President of the rebels of Okoupô. Okoupô gathers all Africans and their customs or that ugliness I call Africaneries.

This dangerous and feared President was not used to receiving people. This is a great opportunity for me to be, in a very sunny afternoon in March, in front of him. In front of my curious eyes, he turns on his satellite phone proudly and calls:

Hello! General! This is your President. Do you understand me?

Yes, very much, Chairman. I hear you perfectly. The telephone connection is fine.

So, tell me what happens during the war on the side A, side B, side C, side D. Tell me how the enemy reacts, how he defends himself, what is his loss of life and what is the extent of damage that your men have caused him. I want to know everything. Make me a complete idea of the current situation on all fronts. I'm listening to you with our favorite journalist.

On all fronts, my men stood firm. I congratulate them. You can be proud of them. They hold the upper hand. They are making steady progress according to my plans. They try to surround, suffocate and weaken the enemy. During the last forty eight hours, they made five hundred prisoners, including twenty generals and fifteen colonels. They killed eight hundred enemies. They grabbed a lot of heavy weapons and much munitions. We destroyed eighteen tanks and we shot down three combat aircrafts. I inform you that tactician General Bakouma and strategist General Doloki have deserted from the enemy and are in exile in Europe. From there, they seek to join us. They send us valuable information on our enemies. With that, we have just easily taken cities like Loada, Yokro, Nouama, Gnaga and Keboua. My President, that serious work was done in just two days by your valiant and brave revolutionary soldiers.

Bravo! Bravo! Thank you, General. All the gods support us in this war. The victory is ours. Today and tomorrow. Forever. Happiness, justice, salvation, freedom and peace are one step away from us. Keep up the heroic march, brave warriors of justice, equality and fraternity. We need next week, at most, the fall down of the rotten, corrupt, xenophobic, racist, tribalic, unjust, tyrannical, cynical, bloody and undemocratic regime of the President Okou. It must fall. Quickly. Very quickly. The country must come back to us. It's our time to govern, to exploit it for our region. It's our time to get rich, to roll in gold and diamonds, to live like rich ones, in the insolent opulence and luxury. It's our time to dominate, oppress, to lie, steal, loot, conspire, to imprison, to divert public funds, to overcharge, to kill and do anything. Yes, anything. I mean anything. Shit! Shit! To each his turn and his time. Every ethnic group its turn and its time. At every region, its turn and its time. By force. This is the law of our country. Isn't it General?

Yes, yes, my President. It's true. It's very well thought out and well said. This is the absolute truth. It's our time to "eat" now and to "sweeten" (it means enjoy the goods and the country's wealth unjustly, arbitrarily, with impunity). I'm in a hurry. Very impatient. Here, in westernized Africa, there is no government working for the people interest. The people don't exist.

We do not govern for all regions and all ethnic groups which are in the stupid, puppet, centralized, dictatorial, tribalized and neocolonial Jacobin nation-state. But we govern only for our own ethnic group, our own area, our parents, our own family, for our own, for our political party. If it is a southerner who is President of the Republic (what a shit Republic!), he rules only for the South. If this is a northerner who is President of the Republic (what a funny Republic!), He rules only for the North. If it is a centrist who is President of the Republic (what a Republic of shit!), He rules only for the Center. If it is a westerner who is in power, he governs only for the West. If it is an Easterner who is in power, he rules only for the East. It's like that. And it will always be like that. Isn't it, President?

Yes, Sir. You're absolutely right. It's always like that. In all neocolonial prisons pompously, ironically, sarcastically and hypocritically called Nations, States, and Republics. It is like that in Côte d'Ivoire. This has led to coups and civil war. That's like that in Ghana. This has led to repeated coups and revolution of John Jerry Rawlings. It's like that in Liberia. This has led to coups and civil war. In Upper Volta, this has resulted in repeated coups and revolution of Thomas Sankara. He has turned his country into Burkina Faso (the country of honest men). In Togo, it has caused repeated coups. In Dahomey, this has resulted in repeated coups and the communist revolution of Mathieu Kerekou also known as Chameleon. He has turned his country into Benin. It's like that in Nigeria. This has led to repeated coups and the Biafra War. It's like that in Chad. This has led to coups and war. It's like that in Central Africa. This has led to coups and war. That's the same situation as in the Belgian Congo. This provoked the war and the revolution of Mobutu Sese Seko, known as Leopard. He has turned his country into Zaire. And his rival, Laurent Desire Kabila, has transformed the Zaire into RDC. It's like that in Congo Brazzaville. This has led to coups and war. It's like that in Niger. This has led to repeated coups. In Mauritania, idem. In Libya, idem. In Gabon, idem. In Cameroon, idem. In Senegal, idem. InGambia, idem. In Sierra Leone, idem. In Algeria, idem. In Tunisia, idem. In Morocco, idem. In Sudan, idem. In Somalia, idem. In Egypt, idem. In Rwanda, idem. In Ethiopia, idem. In Burundi, idem. In South Africa, idem. In Angola, idem. In Guinea Conakry, idem. In Guinea Bissau, idem. In Madagascar, idem. In Mali, idem. In Uganda, idem. InComoros, idem. In Eritrea, idem. In Equatorial Guinea, idem. In Lesotho, idem. The list of these tragedies is long. Too long. It makes me dizzy. I prefer to stop. I hope the world will understand us and prove us right. Isn't it?

Yes my President. Our rebellion to overthrow the apocalyptic power of Okou is fully justified in the eyes of humans. In the eyes of angels. In the eyes of devils. In the eyes of gods. In the eyes of geniuses. In the eyes of our ancestors. I have no regrets to do that. No remorse. No shame. I will continue the struggle until our final victory which is the taking of state power.

Very well, sir. Besides, this victory is not far away. It is at our feet. Since we are stronger. Since we control already 95% of the country. Within only a few days of fighting. We really are stronger, braver, more motivated, smarter, more experienced. In addition we have the support of all Africa, Europe, the almighty John the Butcher (President of the whole American continent), China, Japan, Russia, in short the support of the entire International Community. In addition to all this, our soldiers are everywhere and even in the heart of the regular army of Okou. They constantly tell us the intentions, plans, strategies, tactics and operations of loyalist fighters. 60% of soldiers are loyal to us. They betray the power at any time and sabotage all actions of his army in accelerated decomposition. Long life to the just war we are waging! Long life to our holy war to peace and salvation!

The President of Okoupô rebels, who call themselves the New Revolutionaries, in short, the NR (what funny revolutionaries!), has just talked with his Chief on the phone. What they said is as clear as spring water. This is unequivocal. According to them, they lead the fight for their dignity, their freedom, their happiness, their revenge, their salvation, for justice and equality in their region (Western Okoupô), andfor their ethnic group (the Wouya Wouya of Okoupô). They said that their fight is a fight to get rich too, to live in bourgeois opulence and ostentatious luxury, that it is a struggle to gold and diamond. As do the men in power. Battle in order to exploit Okoupô, dominate, oppress, rob, pillage, plot, do anything as do the leaders of their country. It's a battle of competition in evil. So, their political agenda and the war they make are neither revolutionary nor fair because they are motivated and inspired only by the spirit of revenge and resentment, by hate, envy, jealousy, selfishness and malice. Marxists (disciples of Karl Marx) say they are reactionary (or against revolutionaries). It's dangerous for their poor country suffering already from this shit. I say they are anti-revolutionaries and anti-virtue. Because the revolution (the real one) is rather to condemn and to overthrow a regime and an unjust order that are draconian (which kill freedom), oppressive, exploitationnist in order to build a new society that just gives happiness, freedom, dignity, equality, salvation to all.

The authentic revolution bannishes all evil in the world, any violation of human and citizen rights. The revolution destroyes the evil and establishes the good. It is an expression of beneficial, ascetic, Taoist, Buddhist, Hindu, animist, Christian, mazdeist, wisdom etc.

Any insurrection or subversion (revolt, overthrow) is not a revolution. Cynicism (being inconsiderate, lawless), selfishness, tribalism, nepotism and banditry are not revolutionary behavior. Not at all. The revolution is characterized by self-giving, sacrifice, selflessness, charity, virtuous and glorious deeds.

Okoupô rebels did not understand that. Not at all. They lack the basic socio-political culture. They are rather in a subculture, in a tragic philosophy. They kill and destroy. They are binary and dangerous logic. Logic of violent opposition (thesis-antithesis or action-reaction). They need to enter a different logic. Flexible, dialectic and reconciling logic. Logic or Taoist thinking (thesis-anti thesis-synthesis) that breaks and reconciles rigid positions, which brings together all beings (human, animal, plant and mineral), restores the universal unity, researches the general consensus, peace and universal harmony. The revolutionary dialecticians (those who reject confrontation or violent opposition of two things) advise progress, constantly evolve and not freeze or stabilize. This is the nature of things, beings, ideas and societies. There is no contrary, absolute enemy. There is no good separately (as absolute), no harm separately (as absolute), nofalsehood separately (as absolute), no ugliness (as absolute), no beauty in its own (as absolute), no life separately (as absolute) or death separately (as absolute). Yes, that's like this.

Everything is in everything. All is one and same thing. All is one. Your enemy can also be your friend and rescuer. Everything changes from one moment to another, any state is precarious, any attitude is unstable. Your friend can be your enemy, in certain situations. The good is also evil and evil is sometime good. What is harmful is also useful and what is useful is also bad in other relations. Everything is relative. That's dialectical thinking. You can check around your life and in your daily life. Open your eyes and take notice to people, things, situations and the world.

We go to war to have peace and the return of peace leads to war. Like the day leads to night and the night leads to day. This is the true sense of the world, men and things. If we understand this, we are intelligent and wise. We become cautious. The rebels must learn it. To become true revolutionaries. Good revolutionaries. This will ensure their fame and moral victory over Okou who is both their enemy-friend-brother-fellow.

There is no friend forever and no enemy forever. The rebels tyranny may follow the tyranny of Okou. And peace for all may succeed the tyranny of the rebels. You who want to overthrow President Okou just to perpetuate the same crimes and the same atrocities that you reproach him, are wrong. You are without reason. So study Karl Marx, Buddha, Hegel, Lao Tzu, Jesus, Muhammad, Confucius, Toissin (philosopher, hero and messenger of God Biongon). Frequent the Ivorian philosophers, as Niamkey Koffi, Diby Kouadio, Aka Komenan Landry, who teach the dialectic of Hegel, Marx and Nietzsche, and you will be edified. You will understand your mistakes, your faults, your sins, your mistakes, your illusions, your prejudices. You will understand the absurdity and danger of your dualism (thinking that divides the world into two) and your Manichaeism (the attitude of demonizing others and taking oneself as an Angel). True wisdom will save you.

You want to perpetuate the evil in Okoupô (Okouperies or Africaneries) and freeze it. And you call it revolution. This is notorious ignorance or bad faith. You are indeed the followers, or certified copies of Okou or worse than him. Know that the people of Okoupô expect a radical and qualitative change. A true revolution. Without demagoguery (the act of lying and deceiving the people). Without cynicism (the attitude of someone who is extravagant, without shame, without good character, without civism, who behaves like a dog).

CHAPTER 2

After listening to the President of the rebels of Okoupô and to his Chief of Staff, I continued my restless investigation in my neighborhood. In the capital of Okoupô called Paradise. And always the rebels. On behalf of Toissin this time, I came across a young rebel. No, a former young rebel. His name is Tokonan. He is very popular. He is the curiosity of Soweto area, a paradise ghetto. Tokonan is a deserter rebel. A repentant rebel.

He fled the jungle after escaping death several times. He said he participated in several bloody battles and massacres. He likes to tell anyone who wants to listen to him his exploits and his masterpieces in the domain of evil. His prowess in the field of evil. He likes to show off at any time what he considers as his best war trophy: a human skull painted red and black and very well decorated by him. He has it around his naughty killer's neck to show off. He also has a special cane made with shin of his war deads. His body is covered with horrible amulets. These charms are made with bones, hair and tongues of human corpse. That is the man to whom I handed my own clean and holy micro, one Sunday night, in order to let him talk and confess.

"Let me introduce myself: I am Lieutenant Tokonan. My ethnic group is Bossa. My friends, warriors and rebels, call me Tocard, the invincible. I'm 16 years old. I do not know of White Paper (that means, I am not educated). I did not go to White's school. In my family every body is poor and unfortunate.

I have twelve sisters and nine brothers. My dad and my mom is dead in this war. People here have killed my brothers and my sisters wildly before myself. Mercilessly. They made me drink their warm blood. It made me sick and crazy. After that, I'm become bad, bad, bad. Villain much. Wicked too. I'm still angry. With all the world. With myself too. I'm afraid of myself. I'm too bad. So I killed many, many. Mercilessly. I'm with the rebels there. I kill people there, I drink their warm blood. This is red wine. I eat their raw body. It is braised chicken. It gives me strength, power, luck. We make amulets, fetish, marabout, magic, wizard with that. Look at my neck, my arms, my feet, my belt, it's all gray-gray. It protects me tight against bombs, cannons, machine guns, Kalashnikovs, pistols, twelve gauge, grenades, rockets, knives, machetes of enemy soldiers. That is why I am still living there. My ancestors and the spirits of my house also protect me tight. Every time that I am praying, loud, loud, I shout their names loud, loud. They eat with me. They drink with me. They smoke Ganja, grass (drugs) with me. They give me courage, strong. They love me and they talk to me. They make me invinciblo, invulnérablo, immortally. Immortally here is big, big word. It simply means that someone can not hurt me, can not kill me and I can not die. Never. It is understood that? Okay. When we go to attack Keboua, I was too Daye (I was drugged). We circled the city. Gendarmes, police officers and militaries of Okou have been shot and butchered. Some fled. We raped their women and children many, many. After that we violated all the women of the town. We looted their properties, we broke and burned their houses pretty, pretty there. They burned people who do not like us in their homes. Children were crushed in mortars as Foutou (Ivorian meal). And their parents ate them. I know that my little wild speech is not nice to hear. But I tell it anyway. You must pay attention and understand me well. That's it. I said I'm not gone to school for whites. That's why I talk bad, bad expressions.

I'm not ashamed anyway. I do not care about that. If you are there to laugh at me, I "Gnagne (I do not care, in the Ivorian slang). I have driven many, many people in the wells. They died there and they were really rotten there. I made many, many naughty, naughty things. On behalf of the war. It's called crime not in good language. I am criminal. I am a bandit, murderer, thief, robber, rapist, Ah!

Ah! Ah! It's bad, bad! But it is because of the war. War is not good! God will forgive me. It's not my fault!

I raped white women too much. French, Lebanese, English, American, German, Spanish, Italian… On behalf of the war. Theres no fault. There's no sin. The whites have come there to do what? Only to hurt us. They stole all cocoa from Côte d'Ivoire, all the diamond of the Congo Kinshasa, all the oil from Algeria, Libya. They also stole coffee, timber, gold, iron, uranium, copper, gas, manganese, water, light, air, sun, everything. They killed ThomasSankara, Kwame Nkrumah, Lumumba, Amilcar Cabral, Sekou Toure, Muhammar Kadhafi. They made us slaves, prisoners, colonized, underdeveloped, civilized, and globalized.

All this is bad, bad, bad. They took all our money. We became poor. They laughed at us now. They are thieves, liars, crooks, truants. They also came into our national policy. Ah! God! They dictate us the laws to follow. They impose us President of the Republic we don't like. They impose Prime Minister, ministers, mayors, CEOs, government officials, senators, representatives we don't like. Good God! Bullshit! White is devil, demon, dictator, tyrant, racist, imperialist, colonialist, slavery, AIDS, war, terrorism, danger, pollution, nuclear weapons, xenophobia. They annoy me too much. Enough is enough. I have killed, killed, and killed their children pian! I ate their flesh Pian! I'm too happy. I looted, burned, destroyed their properties, their homes, restaurants, hotels, schools, cultural centers, shops, cars, trucks, airplanes, boats, etc.. I'm too "enjaillé" (happy, happy, in the Ivorian youth slang). I want to see their President, Jacques shit disturber himself here. I will shit in his mouth. He will eat my poo by force. Jacques shit disturber.

I'm going to braise him (burn him alive) as his brothers, his white compatriots braise Africans in France, Italy, America, England… in houses. Why? Why? There's even what? Why White is wicked even like that? For centuries and centuries, for millennia, they attack and attack the black race, the yellow race and the red race. Gift, gift, gift (With impunity). Why does God let White come within Africa? Why God helped white like that? This is not good for us! God is unjust too; schemer too. God is for white only. He is too good for white only. It is White who created God, his God. God is against black. God is against us! The White has destroyed women, children, forest, customs, rivers, oceans, nature, universe. For his science, his technique, his philosophy, his religion and his dangerous politics. Gift. Why? The white has made AIDS, Ebola, avian flu, all the diseases that kill humans. Shit! What they are mad! The Whites destroyed the ozone layer, caused warming of the planet earth. They have polluted the universe, water, air with chemical weapons, atomic, nuclear, with greenhouse gas emissions, with toxic waste. Ivorians are dying now. With impunity. Why?

They have corrupted the entire human species with their rotten civilization, rotten culture, their rotten worldview, and their misconceptions, with their lies, their deceptions, illusions and prejudices catastrophic. The whites have made us criminals, the debauched, the marginalized, the depraved people, rebels, thugs, PDs, lawless people. They turned our women into lesbians, prostitutes. They rendered all crazy. Sick animals and sick people. Crazy chickens, mad pigs, mad cows carnivores, crazy birds. Ah! Damn White! Who wants to control and dominate us by using our own Blacks? It's too clever that. It's too bad that. That way they are masters everywhere and anywhere. They are masters in the Ivory Coast, Burkina Faso, Mali, Senegal, Togo, Benin, Rwanda, Burundi, Liberia, Sierra Leone, Libya, Somalia… Everywhere, everywhere, everywhere.

Whites are making war in Afghanistan, Iraq, Ivory Coast, Liberia, DRC, Sudan, Libya. Everywhere. They spoiled everywhere. They kill everyone. They kill Arabs, Negroes, Indians, Japanese, Vietnamese, Chinese! With impunity. What a danger! They always want to dominate, crush, rob and oppress blacks, Arabs, Yellow and Red. By arms, economics, politics, culture, their languages, their thoughts, their science, their religion, their art, their sport, their philosophy, their technology, their right, their morality, their laws. Anything and everything. They employ all means. And the world looks at them and lets them only do evil.

I, Tokonan, small Negro, dirty, wild, peasant, ex-rebel, ex-revolutionary, dead meat which no longer fears the knife, I spoke here. If it's bad, bad, bad, God forgive me! I abadoned my Kalashnikov. I confessed. I emptied my tummy. I was against President Okou. He is bad, evil, murderer, thief, selfish, unfair, liar, dictator, tribalist. But now as I speak, Mr. journalist, my anger is over! Completely. My hatred is over. Completely. I want peace for my country. I love my country and my country loves me. It's true. It's a draw. I will not destroy it any more. I want national reconciliation. I want the reunification of my country. That's why I left the bush to be here in the capital. Paradise. God bless my dearest country! God save Okoupô! Now, I'll turn to my companion called Pepper. Ex-rebel too. You do not know her. She does not know you either. She is stronger than me. She knows White paper many, many. She's not like me. She has many, many things to say here. She also goes to confession. Listen to him. Sorry, we say listen to her. It's that good language. She is woman. They say "her." They do not say "him." French language is too hard for me. I will learn it after many, many, many in white's school. Listen now miss Pepper."

"Let me introduce myself: I am Miss Mireille Caca. But they call me Sergeant Pepper. On behalf of the war. I am graduated from Law, English and sociology schools. But because of Okou's rotten, corrupt, nepotistic, tribalic, tyrannical and bloodthirsty regime, I'm unemployed, destitute and unhappy. To survive, I have to prostitute myself, to live a life of debauchery, a bitch life and to do anything. I am forced to do anything that is dirty, shameful, degrading, humiliating, destructive and forbidden. I had sex with dogs, with monkeys, with the dead. I am a girl without shame, without faith or law. I am a ruffian, delinquent, brigand, bandit and criminal. In spite of myself. I am the only survivor in my family. Okou soldiers massacred all my relatives under my eyes, without mercy. My father was slaughtered after being riddled with bullets. My mother was raped by ten soldiers before being shot. My five brothers and three sisters were tied up and burned alive in our yard without mercy. I've been raped three hundred times. I was in a coma and I was always violated. At the end, I had become the wife of a Loyalist captain who protected and saved me from death.

After, I murdered him by poisoning and I regained my freedom. That's when I became the first rebellious girl. I took part in every battle. I was on all hot fronts. I was a real butcher at Loada, at Keboua, at Zoulo, and at Tazra. My rings, my necklace, my charms, my earrings, my belt, my shoes, bracelets, my charms are made with human organs, body parts of enemies I've killed. Every day, I drank ten liters of human blood to strengthen me and gain mystical power (magic). It was my coke. The boys call it red wine. So I was invulnerable and invincible in murderer battles and all dangerous operations. I always advance in the fire without fear, bravely, all confident. The enemy does not see me but I see him. I capture and I slaughtered. Thus I have neutralized and destroyed the toughest fighters and greatest strategists and loyalists tacticians. I am Pepper. I put chilli powder in the eyes of enemies defeated and taken prisoners. I am the princess of cruelty and torture. Our pows suffer horribly in my hands. I do suffer some the very painful test of castration. I castrated. I break their balls, I remove their testicles. They bite and swallow. They lose their masculinity. Other are forced to make love to them. They sodomize (they fuck the anus) to bring out their intestines. This is "P.D. test." It's deadly. Other still sleeping among decomposed corpses and caress it. This is "test of death." Still others eat sand, pebbles, gravel, paper, poop etc.. This is "eater test." Still others are hanged, feet in the air and upside down. This is "test of hanging." Ah! Ah! Ah! It is very cruel. Finally, comes the "test of karate": pumps, abs, pecs, endurance, rolls, sweeps, fighting etc. Our prisoners are struggling, struggling and struggling before to die, before being thrown into wells and in mass graves, dead or alive. It's me their supreme judge. I pronounce their condemnation sentence; I decide their ultimate fate. I am their god. I sort and classify them. Those to be beheaded, those to be slain, those who should be shot, who should be skinned and so on. A certain moment, I pretended to leave the rebellion. Then I came back in the government zone. I watched, listened, spied Loyalist soldiers on behalf of the rebels. I even lived with a loyalist Colonel. His name is Pierre JUDO. He madly loved me. He told me many secrets of his camp. I immediately transmitting to the rebels who were exploiting them to thwart and defeat the loyalists. I had always useful information to help, guide and save my fellow rebel attack plans, progress, tactics, strategy, quality of materials, light and heavy weapons of the Loyalists. I am located in the heart of the general information of the State. All decisions taken by the government were laid on the table of my enemy husband. In his absence, I rummaged peacefully in his office. I read all confidential documents, documents containing military secrets. My husband knew nothing of my secret relations with the rebels. He knew nothing of my past. It is a "Gaou" (naive, ignorant, in the argot of the Ivorian youth). We were a total of twenty girls who have infiltrated the regular army by marrying loyalist soldiers. We chatted about losses and continual defeats loyalists in favor of the rebels. But one day, one of us, Françoise called TOTO, was surprised by her husband, when she passed on valuable information to the rebels. She was caught in the act of espionage and intelligence with the rebels. In the army, it is a great crime that is punishable by death. Thus it was shot on the spot by her enemy husband. Mercilessly. Since then, the other girls and me have stopped all direct and active collaboration with the rebels. Fear of being killed."

After these stunning confessions and repentance pathetic these two Okoupô rebel deserters, I am on a Monday morning in the office of an officer loyalist. On behalf of Toissin. This is a longtime friend. There, I recorded joyful news. Exceptional new. Cheerful news of Okoupô.

My eyes curious and inquisitive, my friend picks up the phone to the green color and dials mysterious number.

Hello! General, I am Captain Lucien PANTHERA. Do you hear me? Do you receive me correctly, you say. All right. I have news for you. This is very important. What is it? Well, our chief of staff died. Yes, General Felix HAMMER has just been shot. By General Christian BARBARO. BARBARO was killed in turn by General Jean TIGER. TIGER John was murdered in turn by General Paul SHARK who also died in a fusillade at the Presidential Palace. Entire hierarchy of our republican army is decimated in a few hours. All Generals and Colonels survivors were arrested and imprisoned. Hide yourself well where you are exiled, to have peace. Do contact point with our fellow citizens who are in the same country as you. Is to risk. It is imprudent. You are being watched and highly sought after everywhere.

You were put in several plots to overthrow President Okou. You are tried and convicted in absentia. An international arrest warrant was issued against all officers and exiled opponents. It's the terror and confusion here. It's stalemate. The situation is very confused here. Everyone is suspect. Everyone protects and hides where he can. Private militia of ethnic presidential occupy all the positions left by the deserters, and exiles. Our army is tribalized one hundred percent. Disorder, insubordination and indiscipline are the new virtues of our army. The grunts and militiamen to lay down the law. They reign supreme. They take orders directly to the Presidency of the Republic, with the barons, the caciques and falcons of the regime. They kill and massacre ever. With impunity. They are mass graves here and there. They looted, broken and violent. Nobody can stop them savagely and destroy. They replaced us in all our functions. They decide and do everything for us. There are now several in our armed mercenaries formed by parallel white and black, by private militias and a plethora of pro-government youth associations. These people exercise state power. They hold the effectiveness of state power. No kidding. They are above the law of the republic (what a funny republic!). They have power of life and death over all citizens (what funny people!). On behalf of the war. In the name of the sacrosanct reasons of state. These armies of political party and ethnic group and removed the republican army. By eliminating all the elements belonging to other political parties and other ethnic groups. This is the total ethnic cleansing. The absolute political purge. This is the tribalization frenzied army for the eternal preservation of power. On behalf of the war.

The rebels are advancing constantly and at the gates of our capital, Paradise. They choke us. Mercenaries and militiamen Okou can not resist them nor repulse them. Really, the rebels are stronger, better equipped, more armed than us. They have more ammunition, more courage, more intelligence, more strategies and tactics more than us. They are aided and encouraged by the international community and by impartial forces (how impartial!) That stand between us and them. We are surprised by the lightning advance of the assailants on our soil already too small. This was only possible with the complicity of interposants, neutrals (which neutrality!).

Hello! Captain, can you hear me? Do you copy? Correctly, you say. Very well then. I just received terrible news here. What is it? I teach you that President Okou overturned. Yes, I mean he is overthrown.

By whom? Why? How? Well, it's very strategic. This is a brilliant find. Not to let the rebels take the capital and power, tribalism and radical militiamen led and supported by senior officers and tribalist radicals protecting the regime Okou filed. Nicely. Smooth. This is called coup or putsch Strategic arranged. Okou and is saved from physical death and politics that was hovering above his head. Like the sword of Damocles.

Now it is perfectly safe. Thus the power is still in the hands of people in the East, in the hands of Okou disguised. It will be placed in a safe place. Very, very safe. It will be very well treated, well maintained and easily be able to resume this power later, when the spirits will be calmed. When the country regained its unity and peace. When the North, South, Central, West and East will be permanently reconciled. Okou, the prince of cunning, has been a coup in itself, never fully and finally losing its power to tribal well able to succeed himself. And it is certain that the coup in his service, his pay and his devotion, will a semblance of presidential elections later and then simply resume the power he has temporarily loaned to their stooges and its nominee. What do you think? What I said is it true or false?

It's true. Totally true, Sir. The news was confirmed here. Supporters of radical Okou (ethnics of it) took power. The country is in turmoil. Some laugh, dance, rejoice while others weep, wail and cry up their despair. Some believe they have won everything, while others believe they have lost everything. So goes the world. So true is it that the misfortune of one is the happiness of others. And vice versa.

Okou is no longer President of the Republic. It is no longer Head of State. It is being forced vacation. He is resting. Forced rest. Well deserved. Soldiers are everywhere. Armed to the teeth. It's very impressive. Scary. And terrifying. They took and oversee all strategic points. Such as radio broadcasting, television, airport, port, border, the Presidential Palace, banks, bus stations etc.. Tanks and cargo ships filled with soldiers armed hyper feverishly circulating in the streets. Foreign troops from the UN, ECOWAS, France, America, control and monitor everything. They come and go, phone constantly. Armored battle tanks are exposed everywhere and are ready to spring into action. They graph the Capital Paradise, and help secure people and property, the maintenance of order. Occasionally, government troops shoot bullets into the air (summation). Replicate the impartial forces and take over. Intimidation. Threat. Against looting, violent demonstrations, breakages, the popular uprising. It attempts to dissuade people against a counter coup and chaos.

In its first moments, all putsch raises many anxieties, worries, feelings of doubt, uncertainty, insecurity and fear. This is understandable. And then there was the civil war. This is total disarray. Rumors and wild speculation is rife. People give free rein to their fantasies and their delusions. So we learn here and there that the rebels attacked the capital, they put to flight the President Okou and they took power. Everyone has his comments, its interpretation, its analysis and its lies. By late morning, when radio and television have returned to work after several hours of downtime in their emissions, the world has found the reason. All the gossip ceased incongruous. The truth is then came to light, like a dazzling sun of March. We see, on television, a militiaman lattice, about twenty years old, tall, thin, wearing a cap of General, dyed black in her arms irritated a big Kalashnikov. It is surrounded by a dozen soldiers, grunts and officers alike, very excited. He came to make a statement of great importance. A very solemn and historic declaration.

On behalf of the war and facing extreme danger where Okoupô, and Okoupéennes Okoupéens, dear compatriots, the National Revolutionary Council (CNR), gathering all the patriots and nationalists of all our countries, decided from that moment, change the course of our national history taking and performing for us all state power in order to end the war, the atrocities, the suffering, secession, misery and misfortunes of all kinds. Our country and our people are expensive. Very expensive. Too expensive. We know they need peace, reconciliation, brotherhood, unity, prosperity, development, progress and happiness. In the name of sacred values that are very dear to our homeland and our people that we, CNR, the power to withdraw Sir Charles Okou. Because he failed to realize them. We withdraw it from him power because he has disappointed the hopes and confidence that we all, wherever we are placed in him. On behalf of our salvation to all of us, we are now the new masters of Okoupô. Charles Okou is removed. We will bring order and organization in the country, within three years, general elections are fair, transparent, democratic and open to all countries to give our leaders accountable, legitimate, legal, competent and credible institutions and effective. Meanwhile all this, the National Assembly, the Supreme Court, the Constitutional Council, the Senate, the Economic and Social Council and all other political institutions are dissolved. The constitution is much decried and fought with such ferocity by opponents, by the international community and is suppressed by the rebels. A new constitution will be developed by consensus and voted in a referendum soon. All political parties are dissolved. Put yourself in all our orders. Thank you.

What is said is very clear. What's done is done. The coup against Charles Okou succeeded. The new masters of the country are young people from the presidential movement. It is the young supporters of Okou. Their leader, the new President of the Republic (Republic of shit what!), Is called Adowa (dog language this means gwa Ivory Coast). This name was given the day after his coup. Across the country. This means that it has put a big noose. Better, he got to a terrible noose on which his supporters, the rebels, opponents and the international community will ever make. So he lost freedom. Dog stands for bondage, slavery, havoc, filth, violence and madness.

The coup arranged Okou, his self-coup, Okoupô will plunge into chaos. It's really a coup too. France, sponsor and sponsor coups in Africa, does not accept it. That did not help. This is detrimental to its economic, social, political, cultural and spiritual. The regime of bis Okou, masked and told his guards, his main war dog, Adowa, is very hostile to France. Adowa is a fierce guardian, a fierce defender of Okou and jealous. It is deadly enemy and imperialism, racism, paternalism, and French colonialism. He and his gang have destroyed almost every colonial symbols and all existing property on French soil Okoupô. Adowa was born patriot and nationalist says professional. He is a leader dangerous, an opinion leader uncompromising, a fearsome and dreaded propagandist. As soon as he orders something, his associates, his accomplices and his supporters immediately execute it. They act violently. They break, burn, destroy, molest, pillage, rape, torture and kill. With impunity. Now, here he became President of the Republic (?), Head of State (?). A number of Okoupô. The pattern of anti-French regime, ultra-nationalist, xenophobic. "Ah! Ah! France has hot! ". We hear it and shout loudly in the streets. Everywhere. For men, women, children, dogs, cats, sheep, oxen, roosters, parrots. Yes, the France of Jacques shit disturber, and the Ugly Bread Sokodji hot. Very hot. She trembles with fear. She is humiliated, challenged, dominated and conquered.

She now goes through the UN, AU, ECOWAS to combat Okoupô. His soldiers occupying the country. They are very heavily armed. They are in the air like vultures, vultures, hawks and eagles. Waters like sharks and whales. Ground like lions, leopards, panthers wounded and hungry. They have all the means of mass destruction. They are ready for anything. They are furious and threatening.

But they dare not attack the intrepid warriors and rebels of Adowa. They are hesitant. Loose. They help the rebels and drive them to act. With their valuable assistance, the rebels are very well organized, very well protected and very heavily armed. French and rebels are still together. They work together, eat, steal, loot (gold, diamonds, silver), violent, kill, dance, smoke, chat and play together. French and rebels are friends, comrades and friends.

CHAPTER 3

The French are well illustrated in Rwanda, Congo, Zaire, Central Africa, Burundi, Côte d'Ivoire (with Operation Licorne). They smashed, looted and emptied the agencies of the Central Bank of West Africa (WACB) installed in the cities of Bouake, Korhogo and Man controlled by the rebels led by the student Guillaume Soro Kigbafory. It later became Minister of State for Communications in the national reconciliation government of Prime Minister Seydou Diarra Elimane and, later, Minister of State for the reconstruction and rehabilitation in the transitional government of Prime Minister Charles Konan Banny. Later he became Prime Minister of President Laurent Gbagbo and Prime Minister and Defense Minister Alassane Ouattara of the President. Is this weird? Surprising? No. This is a Bravechè (a good boy in the Bambara language). On behalf of Toissin, I'm always Okoupô. A young French soldier called Rapist is captured by loyalist soldiers. He was taken to the Presidential Palace. There, he underwent torture and closely questioned. His speech is given by the President of the Republic himself, for he confesses, make confessions and revelations useful.

"Let me introduce myself: I'm Sergeant Rapist. I belong to the French military contingent sent to the mission in Okoupô warrior dubbed "Operation Lion." They call me Rapist because more than once, I had to make love to black women genital without their consent and with violence. I like to brutalize women in love. It's my guilty pleasure.

I love making love everywhere and in any manner, to Negro women who do not accept me. It's called rape. So I'm a rapist unrepentant, incorrigible. But I'm not the only blacks to rape women. Most of my colleagues and fellow French soldiers also violates the African women they like with impunity. Every day. They rape black women individually or collectively. They orgy or sailor. On behalf of the war."

Very shocked and hurt in his pride, the President of the Republic suddenly interrupted by a key issue.

Why, the French, do you war against Africans? In Africa? Answer me quickly.

We French, we are at war because we want to openly continue to be happy, rich, powerful, masters, looters, exploiters and rulers of Africa. Because it is good to do that. It is very interesting for us. You know that Africa, your continent, full of riches of all kinds. Africa is a paradise, a paradise coveted by Asians, Europeans, Americans and Pacific Islanders. For us, the French, African countries that we created from scratch by our expansionism (colonization) should remain our perennial plantations, our camps, our provinces, our companions. Forever. Hence we draw at any time, resources and wealth we need for our greatness, our power, our happiness, our progress, our salvation and infinite development. Given these economic, social, political and strategic, we can not accept you, Africans, you chassiez your continent and your country are our products, our products, our colonies. For us, the French colony is a colony and it must remain colony. Forever.

Still very angry, President Adowa asked a second question no less serious;

But one thing seems strange and paradoxical. France has said already developed, rich, powerful, great. I do not understand why she still needs Africa, property and wealth, to the point of making war to maintain its domination in all directions (in all senses) on it. I'm listening.

I know that Negroes are not intelligent. But, for once at least, try to understand, Your Excellency of my ass, that France can not do without Africa. France saw only neo-colonialism, that is to say the uncontrolled exploitation of its colonies. It is very easy to understand. Even by fools and dunces absolute. For example, we own all your assets: gold, diamonds, manganese, iron, uranium, bauxite, coffee, cocoa, pineapple, banana, rubber, wood, etc. ... We sell you all. You do not manufacture anything. We do everything for you. You are spoiled babies. You expect all of us, your teachers and your eternal gods. All your properties belong to us. I quote the most prestigious Presidential Palace, National Assembly, Treasury, Economic and Social Council, Administrative Tours. It is we who have built everything here. At any instant, each Okoupéen enriches us by working for us, buying something, sleeping in a house, dressing, eating anything from cigarettes, drugs, drinking water, liquors, dyes, by moving in cars, trains, planes, boats, breathing air, oxygen, speaking our language, writing, communicating, reading, being knowledgeable and fun, relaxing etc.. You contribute to the influence and the greatness of our nation and our culture. How? By following our values blindness, slavishly imitating all our ways and customs, trying to civilize you like us, you as we develop, democratize you like us, you as we globalize, get married like us, talk like us, think like us, as we give birth, as we live, we die like, look like us, you govern like us, as we produce, as we sleep, to dress like us, eat like us, as we instruct you, as we communicate, smoking like us, as we drink, as we write, as we read, as you inform us, as we relax, make war like us, you rebel like us, as we do of terrorism, as we go on strike, making revolutions like us, as we practice the dictatorship, tyranny, like us, Jacobinism and despotism (formation of a unitary, centralized) like us, as we lie and cheat, making demagoguery like us, ness shots of State like us, your prostitute women like us, pervert people like us, as we brigander, pollute the atmosphere like us, you poach as we practice selfishness and individualism as we, like we practice modernity. Finally, do you understand something, Excellency the President of my white ass White? I must admit frankly that it is not at all easy to understand something of the Niggers. Y there another question?

Yes, of course, white boy, soldier-warrior-lion of my ass black Black, black beard of my Black. Patience! The intelligence that you refuse to recognize me lets me know that you are a dead meat that is not afraid of a knife. You are addicted and you are now, crazy. You are crazy and ready to die without feeling anything. You know very well that you will not get out alive of this Palace. So I will allow you to spit your raw truths and offensive. I allow you to spit your venom all racist and imperialist and say anything that might offend, shock, outrage and offend a Head of State, a sensitive personality, irascible (who may be angry) like me. Keep it up. It's good for you. I encourage you a lot in that. Do you understand me, warrior, soldier, raving mad?

Watch yourself. Empty your stomach and your mind angry and belligerent. You have nothing to lose or maintain here. I want your already miserable life of a lion in my black ass Black in hand. I am about to drink my earlier bandji (wine extract from palm oil) in your skull white White, who will be my king and my cup trophy of war. Trophy of war against France racist, and imperialist demonic Jacques shit disturber, and the Ugly Bread Sokodji. White boy, dead meat arrogant, insolent, impudent, cynical, this is my third and final question, before they kill you.

You just said, just now, that we, Africans, slavishly imitate the West, we know nothing else to do, that's very dangerous for us. I agree that this remark is quite right. But then, tell me, if I have reason to fight imperialism, racism, paternalism and neo-French, to claim complete and absolute independence for my country. Clearly, I want to know if I have to kill you and kill all the French present in my country, and revolutionize Okoupô release. What does France expect from me exactly? You have the floor. I'm listening.

I say no, no and no. You must not do that. This is absurd. Very stupid. This is suicidal. You can not get your dignity, your happiness, your hello there. War, killing, the revolt against France will not give you freedom, greatness, glory, peace, security and prosperity. Quite the contrary. You will be annihilated. You will lose everything. Try a little and give me reason. France, the powerful France, my country will not tolerate any violence by you against it. All your land will disappear in a minute. And imperialism, racism and neo-French survive and thrive forever. All African countries and their leaders may disappear from this world in one minute if they try to decolonize strength or resistance to French imperialism. But the great France, la belle France and the mighty France who loves liberty, equality, justice and fraternity for his son and daughters white, will continue his glorious humanitarian mission of democratization, civilization, rescue, globalization, defense of Human Rights and Citizens across the world. Alongside its American allies and

English. It was France who decides everything for you. It is France that is your destiny. It was she who created you in His image. It can destroy what it has built. Nobody can stop him. It manufactures Presidents of the Republic for Africa and the removal of power when it sees fit, when they are not his will. When these Presidents are rebelling against it and act against its interests. Read a little recent history of Africa and see if moult edifying of our power and dominating destabilizing the puppet states, puppets that we created from scratch. You must know what is happening now in Ivory Coast, Togo, Benin, Chad, Congo, DRC, Libya, Tunisia, Egypt, Morocco, Algeria, Guinea Conakry, Gabon, Senegal, Mali, Burkina Faso etc.. It has a glorious name. This is the France- Africa. The France-Africa is denounced, criticized and condemned by our opponents imperialists, by our enemies and our victims. And this is normal. I fully understand the complainants. It is their absolute right and sacred duty. The reggae singers like Alpha Blondy, Tiken Jah, Serges Kassy, Ivory Coast and many others have reason to complain, to attack us through their political songs. But that's all they can do. This can only set us back a step. No. The France-Africa remains. It progresses with its corollary the Francophonie. You, President Adowa, you owe us all: your hundred days in office, your poor Negro life, money to pay your slaves of servants, your weapons, your Presidential Palace, your castles and sumptuous villas here and of France, your cars, your planes, your boat, your trains, your health, safety, etc.., etc.., etc. … So you quickly submit to the will of the French authorities. Jacques never said no shit disturber, Vilain Pain, Sokodji is being stupid, arrogant and ungrateful. Submit yourself quickly to the will of France if you want to continue living, to govern, to enjoy your countless ill-gotten gains, your privileges excessive, improper and unjustified your many prerogatives. Finally, submit yourselves to the will of French if you want to be at peace, safe and happy. This also applies to your boss, Charles Okou, which is currently hidden behind you. Be smart and careful. Poor negro, negro, négrion, cooperate with the mother now France. Make peace with France. Be loyal to France and run all his orders, all his dictates to the letter, with zeal, loyalty and devotion. Your name is Adowa. You're a dog. For us, Francaix, the main qualities of the dog are the absolute loyalty and continued friendship with his master. For that alone, he owes his happiness and his salvation. You and your boss, Okou, must follow this great example of dog. Be of good dogs happy in shackles and chains.

Gladly accept your fate of colonized natural and eternal spoiled dogs. Keep quiet and docile. Under these conditions only there, France is committed immediately to protect you, to enrich you and let you die in power by reducing the rebels to nothing, in reuniting Okoupô and by bringing peace in three days. Okou will comfortably reinstalled in his position as President of the Republic and Head of State. If they wish. You, Adowa, will be his Prime Minister. If you wish. Come on, I listen.

Sergeant, I am very relieved, comforted and very happy to hear this speech friendly and brotherly of you. I am really excited. I believe that peace is now possible between France and Okoupô. Any misunderstandings between you and us are dispelled. A new and beautiful rises on the world and Okoupô. The days of hope, mutual trust and bilateral cooperation between beneficial and meaningful the French and Okoupéens, between your country and ours. In the background, and in reality we are not anti-French revolutionaries. We have absolutely nothing against the great France, nothing against la belle France who created us in His image and glory that has trained us to serve loyally. The French President is our brother, our friend and our true President here in Okoupô. We are its employees and servants here. We can only love him, respect him and obey him. Our violent reactions in recent times are only due to your pretend neutrality and your pretense of impartiality in the management of the terrible crisis in our country and our system, that is to say the war we are waging against the rebels. This has confused and terrified. Frankly, we would have liked the great France was openly on our side, that we might be with him openly and directly to quell the rebellion and win the war on behalf of the defense agreements between our two countries. But, alas! This was not the case. We had the painful feeling of being abandoned and betrayed by our motherland what la belle France. I admit that we were very disappointed and frustrated. Now, all this is repaired. Everything is entered in the order. God, thank you! We are now reconciled. Forever.

France will remain our only trading partner in the world. We give back to him, today, all our markets. Alone will do everything for us.

All that has previously been given to China, Japan, Russia, Korea, USA, Canada, Germany and India will be withdrawn in favor of France. We will train no more engineers, technicians, teachers, doctors, administrators and national frameworks. Those already working here will be retired prematurely. We look urgently for volunteer and French technical assistants. My country will abandon its revolutionary Okoupô name (or the country that kills, language Gwa Ivory Coast). It will resume its former name. Its colonial name that is neutral and peaceful Earth diamond. My boss will abandon his revolutionary name and warrior Okou (death). Soon there will be ministers, deputies, mayors and senators to Okoupô French. All department heads, all of our CEOs, our central directors, all our consultants, our chiefs of staff and all our chiefs of staff will now be the French.

There will no one French Ministry of Culture and Ministry of Francophonie Okoupô. The French army will take the place of our national army. All our soldiers and our militia be disarmed, demobilized and reintegrated into the economic fabric. They will cultivate the land, produce food, catch fish, hunt animals, work in factories, playing football and playing music. Ministries of economy and finance, defense, security, mining, agriculture, national education, culture and foreign affairs will return to France. We do not want more independence or sovereignty. Does it can go like that, my Sergeant?

Yes, very well. Ah! Ah! Ah! You do good servant of the devil. We ask you and you give a thousand we ask you and you give everything. But finally, it proves that you understood everything, now that you are intelligent and wise. So everything will change favorably for you. Okou will be president for life. You, Adowa, you will be Prime Minister for life. Peace has now returned to Okoupô. Reconciliation of your country is already done. The rebellion against you is over. Your development is underway. Democracy is already running here. The Rights of Man and Citizen are very well respected here. Okoupô globalization is a total success. Your constitution will be amended to the need of the case as was done in Togo for the old Eyadema, Gabon in favor of the old

Bongo, Burkina Faso for Blaise Compaore and Ivory Coast for Bédié of Robert Guei and Laurent Gbagbo against Alassane Ouattara. We will reduce all your enemies and your opposition into silence. We calmerons AU, EU, ECOWAS and the UN. One moment, please! I have a phone message from my minister of colonization and the France-Africa. I answered quickly in two words: "Hello! Dear Mr. Minister, I receive you very well. That is understood. In addition, I inform you that I am currently at the Presidential Palace of Okoupô. For an interview very, very productive meeting with President Adowa. Everything is settled amicably here. Plan A worked. You know what I mean. Inform, your turn, once the President of the Republic so that it cancels the plan B. Its application will be useless and harmful. You know what I mean. Finish."

Back on topic, President. You, on your side, immediately inform your boss Okou. Tell him that his troubles are over now, that all problems are resolved in his favor, he will find his Chair in the hours after our conversation today, he is about to make statements Okoupô of the nation, he prepares his next coup posts. This is how it goes. Go, tell him in my presence.

All right, Sergeant. I call it. 'Allo! Excellence is President Adowa. The news I give you are very good and very promising. Take good notes of everything I say and run it immediately. Your beautiful dream is realized here. Indeed, I spoke here at the Palace, with a representative of the city on all points of contention and problems are resolved in amicable in our favor. Get ready to take over the reins of power. There will be a new coup arranged, a semblance of coup, a real fake coup in the hours that follow. It will be in your favor. I give you the power and I take the place of Prime Minister. I just signed a new deal very colonial, very interesting. Prepare your messages already, your statements to the nation according to the protocol in use. Done."

Sergeant Knife, aka Rapist, before letting you leave here, I want to thank you most sincerely on behalf of my country, on behalf of the President and Okou for myself the beautiful work you've done for me, and for Okou Okoupô. I will never forget you. For, thanks to you, I can finally breathe, eat, sleep and live in peace, You are not a toy soldier, a sergeant or a mere vulgar rapist. But you are a great natural diplomat who knows save a country from chaos. You saved my country from death. My people you will always be very grateful. Tomorrow, you will be decorated, honored and glorified by myself. You will be made a Knight of the Order of Merit of the Republic of Okoupô. You deserve such a distinction is a moral reward. But, today, already, hold five billion CFA francs to pay for your transportation. Take also this little bag containing a little diamond and some gold. Thank you again. Thank you very much and goodbye!

That's it. It goes again. The wrong way. On the wrong path. By a dangerous shortcut. A new pact between the colonial authorities okoupéennes and the French authorities. Commitments are made of either side. For a diabolical cooperation for the benefit of France and in the selfish interest of leaders Okoupô. On behalf of threats, intimidation, corruption, paternalism, blackmail, France-Africa (French side) on behalf of selfishness, megalomania (delusions of grandeur), cowardice and of imbecility (okoupéen side). The Negroes of Okoupô have proved that they are feeble-minded, cowardly, stupid, dominables, fearful and corruptible as desired. The whites still on a roll (all they succeeded). They still have the lion's share. They always have the spotlight. With the Negroes, they win big. They earn everything. They give an egg to get a bull, an elephant. A fool's bargain. In Africa, while they can. This is the status quo. Adowa Adowa rest. The dog never changes his way of sitting. It is well known. It is proverbial. Legendary. The dog remains faithful to his master, to his boss. Even if the boss is wrong, wicked and cruel towards her. Dog is dog. Allotted is allotted (in dog language Agni of the Ivory Coast). Wourou is wourou (dog Bambara language). Amon is amon (dog language Aboure Ivory Coast). Gba is GBA (in dog language Ebrie Ivory Coast). The game is still good for white people cynical and racist. Okoupô and all its wealth of all kinds are assigned, sold off to white greedy, insatiable and who dream of taking advantage of the moon, Mars, Venus, Jupiter, etc.., Etc.., Etc.. Binary logic (thinking that pits two terms) of domination is still running against all non-whites. But, in particular, against the Negroes who still prefer to resign. Afghans attacked and invaded by the coalition racist, imperialist, terrorist and evil whites, continue to fight fearlessly. They continue to strenuously defend. In the same vain, the Iraqis attacked and invaded by the same coalition to defend white madly. And they will eventually win the war, for liberation from Western occupation. Similarly the North Koreans, who are still threatened and torpedoed by America and its lackeys Asian defend themselves and resist admirably well. They even defy all the imperialists. They avoid the pitfalls western coated with gold and diamonds that have the names; Democracy, Globalization, Human Rights and the Citizen, Food, Development, Modernity, Wealth, Growth, etc. Progress. Cobi! Covan! (Con dirty! Con rotten language Baule of Côte d'Ivoire).

Here in Africa, only Muammar Gaddafi (enlightened guide and inspirer of the Libyan revolution) and Robert Mugabe (the warrior, the father of independence and the strongman of Zimbabwe) do well. All right. They know how to defend against imperialism and its seductive traps. They know how to enforce. They have withstood whites predator-vampires (thirsty of Africa's wealth). They resist heroically all their threats, all their penalties, all their attacks, their bullying, their blackmail, their attempts at bribery and seduction. Bravo! Glory to them! Glory to their bravery and their heroism! Let this be an example to other Africans, especially the youth of our continent. The youth will have the difficult task of continuing the same battle and win. May the example of Gaddafi and Mugabe do school. That Gaddafi and Mugabe have many imitators, many imitators and many imitators.

But besides these two exemplary personalities, as do other Negroes, other Heads of State and their people niggers? Are they cursed? Are they doomed by evil gods to live forever in nègreries and négrailleries shameful and humiliating? Are they cursed into accepting the unacceptable, slavery, imposed on them until the end of time? Really, really, there is reason to be surprised. There is nothing to worry about. What despair of the Negro. A when the end of the nègrerie? The niggertrash? The négraillerie? Strongly change! And fast! At the earliest!

CHAPTER 4

The news came. At five in the morning. The President of Adowa, was overthrown by the Mafia led by Bob Bernard. To the surprise of the people of Okoupô. RFI, BBC, AFRICA N° 1 and the Voice of America commenting on the event extensively. For special editions. Okou regained power. By a coup. Velvet. Without violence. Without bloodshed. This is a coup well arranged. An imperialist plot. Neocolonialism and French. This is denounced. Criticized and condemned. Forcefully. By the political opposition, the rebels, ECOWAS, the AU, EU and UN. In the streets of the capital Okoupéenne, Paradise, excited crowds break, burning vehicles and buildings. They kill whites and foreigners. They violate and slay their wives. The Embassy of France is sacked and fired. The French Cultural Center was burned. Schools, hospitals, factories and various French companies are destroyed. At the speed of light. The French army, which is deployed throughout the country, firing live rounds at the people okoupéen. The cannons roar. Shells and bombs explode. Grenades, Kalashnikovs, rockets and other lethal weapons are heard. Everywhere. Okoupéen revolted against the people, the danger and terror Franco-UN are present. The sky is filled with their helicopters and other monstrous bombers. Waters (lakes, lagoons, Atlantic Ocean) are occupied by their sailors and submarines terrifying. On land, they are the same hellish battle scenes.

Ambulances and hearses French military Okoupô crisscross the capital. In all directions. To collect the millions of corpses who will find themselves in mass graves and mass graves. Genocide. Massacre as in the Franco-Algerian war where there were a million dead. A million

Algerians killed in Algeria. Who wanted freedom. Independence. Justice. Dignity. Happiness.

A Okoupô, there are three million deaths. Okoupéen side. And one hundred people killed. On the French side. In a week of clashes. For Okoupéens is Calvary. The Apocalypse. Okoupô, is Iraq. This is Afghanistan. Its capital, Paradis, who was once gay, cheerful, smiling, became sad and gloomy. It is now a vast cemetery. This is Baghdad. Kabul. Algiers. Iroshima. Nagasaki. Great France, beautiful France, which loves Liberty, Justice, Equality, Fraternity, the Human Rights, Democracy, is now showing his true greatness (greatness in evil. Smallness moral). And its true beauty (the beauty in evil. The moral ugliness). It shows she loves Liberty for the French alone, Justice for the French alone, only the Equality between the French, the only Fraternity among the French, the Human Rights for the French alone. Democracy for the French alone. Man with large H, universal man, that is, basically, the only French. Rights with its large D are, basically, Rights of the French alone. His dignity is, basically, the dignity of the French. Okoupeanus homo (man of Okoupô, okoupéen the citizen, in Latin) is an animal, a thing, an object. Civilization with a capital C, Universal Civilization, is basically the only French civilization. Ah, what a cunning imperialist! Modernity is, basically, the only modern French. Democracy could not be found elsewhere, outside of France and the West. All that is good is white. And all that is bad is not white. Good is white, evil is non-white. The white is true, the false is non-white. That is Manichaeism (a way of seeing things that divides people into good and bad) delusional. It is also of solipsism (the attitude of those who think it's the only one to exist) delusional. We also call it narcissism (self-admiration, self- aggrandizement pathological).

The thinker Montesquieu said it was necessary for whites to treat blacks as inferior beings or as animals so they can enslave and colonize without problem. Because their Christian religion prohibited them from doing harm to men (see the Ten Commandments). The Christian religion, whose claim to whites, forced to respect the dignity of human beings and recognize that all human dignity. Whatsoever. To work around this divine obligation, whites had to lie. They had to distort the blacks in their minds by treating them as beasts, to be at peace with their religious conscience. To escape the divine sanctions. Thus Jesus Christ blesses and protects the white killers, murderers, looters, exploiters and oppressors of Africans because they are blacks like animals. Bravo! To Christianity! Good ideological support (support of ideas, thoughts) for the crimes and evil. Because it allows evil against the animal kingdom (except man), against the mineral kingdom and against the plant kingdom. It denies dignity, spirit and life to these beings there. This is very dangerous. For the Negro, these beings treated as discredited, deserves to be abused. As for African animism, Hinduism, Buddhism and Taoism Asian, all being and all things deserve respect. For these religions there, the animal, plant and mineral are equal to men (in rights and dignity). They should not be abused, destroyed or removed from the world. Best, these religions teach man that it forms a fundamental unity, a coherent and consistent with these beings there. It depends on these beings and these beings are dependent on him. So there is interdependence, unity and solidarity and ontological nature (that means in their constitution or in the idea we have of it) between man and all that is not human. All is one and the same thing. Who knows where the human begins and where it ends? So do not despise any being underestimated in the universe, in nature and the world. Africans and Asians are right. They feel better than whites. We must now think and act Animist and Taoist. You should know that everything is in everything. In the great All. Destroying part, is to destroy everything (and universal harmony) and destroy it all, is to destroy a party. Every being exists only in light of other beings (its complement) and vice versa (individual- society; day- night life- death, small- large; element-together). The Yellow, Red and Blacks know the truth of the world. They are intelligent and wise. The white man is ignorant and foolish. He has much to learn from the Black, Yellow and Red. He must learn in non-whites. To be intelligent. Sage. Human. But despite that, the White denigrates, mockery, scorn and insult non-whites. It is totally lacking in humility and honesty. He said while it is truly greater than. It is superior in stupidity. In ignorance. In follies. Evil. Only. What glory! This is the opinion of my friend Roger Garaudy. This is a white man. French.

He is honest. Reasonable. Sage. He became a Muslim. This is a great intellectual. A Philosopher. A true philosopher. A humanist. Is it any wonder? He was educated Africans, Asians, Europeans, Americans... He compared the African civilizations and cultures to cultures and civilizations of other continents.

It's called dialogue of cultures and civilizations. He condemned the Western culture and civilization too materialistic, atheistic, warlike, savage, barbaric and imperialistic. It is anti-racist and anti-Eurocentric. This means it is against injustice, arbitrariness and the hegemony of whites. It is humanistic. He knows, respects and loves everyone. Especially non-whites. I stay Okoupô only. Despite the confusion and havoc general Okou ordered his Prime Minister, Adowa, to form an emergency government of public salvation (GSP). The new government consists of strange people. Exceptional. Very exceptional. This is unheard of in Okoupô. Throughout Africa. And worldwide. Moreover, Okoupô changed its name. It is now called, Earth Diamond. This is his original name. The colonizer that its founder gave it. Because of its immense wealth in diamonds. And indeed, there is this diamond which is now his misfortune. The abundance of goods is sometimes harmful. The diamond Okoupô are coveted too. He is played by the world. Hence unrest and war. About odd government of Tierra Diamond, note a fact. Besides the President and his Prime Minister, all other members are women. Yes, women. Only women. Why? Well, Okou and Adowa are fans of women too. Too in love with women. Beautiful women. Of beautiful babes. Of any country. Okou twenty women for himself. Twenty healthy women counted in his harem. Forgiveness in his home. Adua, his rival, has thirty to himself. I mean thirty. No kidding. The President and Prime Minister of the Earth are Diamond maniacs. They have a mania for women. Like all other African leaders. Felix Houphouet-Boigny of the Ivory Coast, nicknamed the wise man of Africa, were several women. Mobutu Sese Seko of Zaire had several wives. Even twin sisters. Laurent Gbagbo of Côte d'Ivoire were several women. Our presidents and our African Heads of State have all, without exception, very low for the fairer sex. They have a very low to the called weaker sex. They are all womanizers. Of Don Juan and satyrs.

This is how many beautiful and charming girls entered the new government Okou. Minister of Education: Djantra miss Claudine (Associate Professor of Law). Minister of Justice and Keeper of the Seals: Delphine miss Claman (magistrate). Minister of Information: Puppy miss Augustine (civil engineer). Defense Minister: Êtinvê miss Bernadette (associate professor of history). Minister of Internal Security: Djandjou miss Josephine (doctor). Minister of Economy and Finance: miss Djougouya Jacqueline (lawyer). Foreign Minister: miss Blate Françoise (doctor) etc.., Etc.., Etc.. What does it say these ministers? These are all brains. Body of well-made and well-filled heads. Women barred with scholarly credentials. Expected of them much good. Many miracles. Nothing but miracles. Things that men could not be ministers in all previous governments. These women are condemned to leave their country of darkness, and hell to save him. This is their challenge. They must succeed where men have failed. They must fix men, recreate, transform, purify, sanctify them. Is it not women who put men in the world? They therefore have a duty to educate them to make the angels and gods. Otherwise, they bear the responsibility for failures and mistakes of men. Is it not true that men often act on behalf of women? All human actions are designed to bring happiness and pleasure for women. It is for the welfare of women than men work, steal, kill and wage war. This is for the woman that the man does good or evil. This is the ultimate explanation of the war and rebellion to Okoupô.

For women the money has no smell, no color. Money is money. It is everywhere and always helpful. Whatever its provenance. Regardless of its owner. Money a devil equals money from an angel. The money from a thief is equal to the money of a saint. And all money is dirty. He is still ill-gotten land in Diamond. It is the product of crime, crime, evil, cheating, corruption, prostitution, homosexuality, exploitation, theft etc.. About the Government feminized Earth Diamond, I ask myself a question. I wonder how this harem of Okou manage to save Okoupéens. This is to resolve problems like: war, rebellion, secession, imperialism, racism, colonialism, neo-slavery, mismanagement, bad governance, corruption, nepotism, tribalism, decadence, misery popular AIDS, dictatorship, globalization, prostitution, homosexuality, racketeering, state terrorism, moral depravity, perversion human, coups, crime, insecurity, unemployment, impunity, violence, anarchy, and political unionism in school, white school year. The people of Okoupô has placed all his confidence and all his hope in these women ministers.

After spending five years at the helm of the country, they are accountable to the people. They must be judged. What is their positive contribution? Where are the miracles expected of them? What is the GDP (gross domestic product) present in the country? What is the current growth rate of the nation? The rate of evil, which was 98%, he declined? Rate well, which was 1% has it increased? How much? The unemployment rate, which was 86%, he declined? How much? The rate of development, which was 1%, he rose? How much? What is the rate of happiness for the country? What is the sign of salvation for the nation? The latest report of investigations Okoupô by the international community gives the alarming figures: the annual per capita income is a CFA, the growth rate is 10%, the rate is 100% wrong; rate well is 00%, the unemployment rate is 96% development rate is 00% of happiness is the rate of 00%, the rate is 00% hello; morality rate is 00% and the rate of religiosity is 00%, the rate of political legality is 00%, the rate of political legitimacy is 00%, the rate of 00% is democracy, the practice rate is 00% Republican, and the rate is 100% evil, the freedom rate is 00%, the rate is 00% Justice, truth is the rate of 00%, the rate of lying was 100%, the rate of bad faith is 100%, the rate of violence is 100% the rate of fraternal equality is 00% rate of good citizenship is 00%, the rate is 100% anarchy, crime rate is 100%; the crime rate is 100% delinquency rate is 100%, the rate of prostitution is 100% the rate of homosexuality is 95%, the rate of sexual promiscuity is 100% the rate of sexual perversion and eroticism is 100%, the rate of moral depravity is 100%, the rate of gangsterism is 100%, the rate of single women is 97%, the survival rate is 1% and the rate of patients was 98%, the rate of HIV (AIDS) is 100% the poverty rate is 99%, the rate of ignorant, illiterate, 98% are illiterate; beggars rate is 98%, the rate of school dropouts is 96%, the rate is 70% slavery and the unhealthiness rate is 100% the rate of hunger is 98%, the rate of terrorism is 100%; the rate of white school year is 95%, the rate of wild strikes is 90%, the rate of pollution in the country by toxic waste is 100%.

That is the record of glorious women ministers, technocrats. This is the work of girls, the "gos" of "medals" (women in the slang of the Ivorian youth). That the grandiose and magnificent government Okou bis bis government following a coup arranged. Shit! Fucking hell!

Bullshit! Amonbin (cunt of your mother language Gwa Ivory Coast). What do you want me to say across Okou (death, language Gwa)? Of his harem and his rotten regime by selfishness, banditry, and neo-imperialist conspiracy, by tribalism, nepotism and feminism? Hold! All women are friends of ministers Okou and Adowa. They are masters of these two men cursed and rotten (they share their beds with them). So are really most African Heads of State. They are not disinterested, altruistic or own. Far from it. They do not choose their ministers, their managers, their advisors and ambassadors at random for their skills, citizenship, or loyalty to their efficiency and expertise. They did that shit about these qualities. The key is for them to earn what they need. Their personal interests. They do not bother with morality, law, religion, science or philosophy binding ascetic.

Their only course of action is cynicism, that is to say the dog's life. The life of Adowa. They excel in evil. They are champions in trouble. Their rate is 100% wrong and their rate of property is 00%. And they do not feel ashamed. Instead, they are very proud. They rejoice. For them, it is glorious. Virtuous. They transvalue all values. That means they have transformed ordinary morality, asceticism (rigorous exercise) and religious. Adua and his boss are real dogs Okou (cynical). They eat in the garbage. They are all dirt, filth in all, in all the ugliness and all villainies. They were men empty. Lackluster. Without grandeur. Okoupô (either home or country of death, language Gwa Ivory Coast) looks like all African countries in ugliness, dirt, in disorder, violence. All cities compete with African capitals. Especially with Abidjan, the economic capital of Ivory Coast. They are rotten like Abidjan, shit. As Abidjan, the queen of inadequacy, of disorder, insecurity and death. Rotten as the Rue Princesse Yopougon in Abidjan. City of evil, disorder, all the vices and all the crap. Rotten as Abobo and Adjame Renault,

Treichville, Marcory, Kumasi, Port-Bouet, Plateau, Zone 3, Zone 4, etc. Cocody. All this is Abidjan. These are districts of Abidjan. There are Princes and Princesses of evil. Earth as Diamond. I talk about policy Okoupô. Yet. Always. This is my only job, that. It was believed that women ministers Okou had better ministers than men. For since its founding in 1845 by white settlers, until Okou bis Okoupô was governed only by chih (boys Bambara language). It was believed that the Bla (female language Baule of Ivory Coast) could succeed where the Yassoua (boys Baule language) failed). It was believed that the Bla would accomplish extraordinary things. But, alas, this is totally the opposite that we have seen. Of the Bla Okou are not the Amazons of Dahomey King Behanzin. They are not the intrepid warriors and heroines. They are all just good to use bed sheets to Okou. To satisfy the libido (sexual desire, love instinct) of Okou. But they are not up to the Herculean tasks they were assigned. They have disappointed the people okoupéen. They have not solved one of its many problems. They are unworthy. Totally unworthy the confidence of the people. They were too much honor useless. Ministers of my ass. They have only to demagogic rhetoric, misleading, feminists and sterile. They played the loudmouths. This is unique to women educated, wealthy, westernized and liberated "from" Okoupô. Emancipation of my ass. Politically, they are completely disqualified. They are more miserable than the most seedy seedy men. They are envious, jealous and embittered men they regard as their opponents, rivals, competitors and enemies. They spent all their time to punish, to correct men and avenge them. Then they looted, ransacked and looted and the country's wealth. They roll on gold and diamond. They roll carriages. They roll the bigger machines. Shiny and brand new. Mercedes, BMW, Jaguar, Porsch, Chevrolet, Limousine, Ford etc.. They have buildings, villas and castles of gold, marble and diamond. Factories, enterprises and plantations. The gos (women in the Ivorian slang) have it all. Anything and everything. They did everything. Anything and everything. Unless the duty. Namely, the duty to save the school down, to save the millions of unemployed, millions of them as prostitutes, the poor and destitute. The duty to combat pollution, toxic waste (from abroad to enrich them), killing everyone. The duty to reunite and pacify the country, to reconcile Okoupéens (brothers became enemies), to remove the French imperialism and neocolonialism, to restore order, security and rebuild a new African state free, independent, powerful and prosperous. They paraded. They have the flashy. They crushed the men by invective (very aggressive speech), jousting (verbal fight, quarrel) oratories to relent feminist, by their material acquisition, enrichment cynical (dog policy), by arbitrary decisions, eccentric, tyrannical and sexist. According to their numerous ministerial orders, it is only necessary for women in parliament and head of all republican institutions. Amonbin! (Your mother's cunt, Gwa language of Côte d'Ivoire). Republic of my ass! They also require that married men make the market and the kitchen instead of their wives. They drink pee and eat the excrement of their wives. To prove their love for them. Whether made enceinter by their wives and they give birth in lieu thereof. That's democracy and the Republic of Women Ministers and sexist feminist Okoupô. Bravo! The gos! That is revolutionary. Revolution in my ass! This is unusual. Tyrannical. It is modernity. Modernity of my ass! This is the total subversion. Diabolical. Amonbin! (Your mother's cunt, Gwa language of Côte d'Ivoire). Shit! Shit! Shit shit!

CHAPTER 5

With women in power, the crisis continues okoupéenne. It gets worse. This is the greatest misfortune. The greatest danger. Okoupô women ministers are irresponsible. Crazy. They have spoiled everything. These brothels have plunged the Earth into darkness Diamond and total deadlock. Animated by an instinct sexist and feminist unsavory and distasteful, they decided that men love (the proper sense of that word) women. They allow themselves to crush, dominate, exploit and ridicule by women. They ordered, and decreed stopped the tyranny of the woman. The féminocratie. This means that women now wear pants okoupéennes and the men wear the kodjos (cache-African female). Disaster. Women ministers have lost the North (the reason). This is not without consequences, without inconvenience, safe. Brothels President Okou revolted and the entire population, all male chauvinists (anti-feminist) and all the peasants. They pissed on customs. On the traditions. And African sacred taboos. They trampled and violated the fundamental laws of Africa. They put the country in turmoil, at risk. This is total confusion. Fucking hell! Cobi! Covan! (Con dirty, rotten con, language Baule of Côte d'Ivoire).

The entrance to the villages is now prohibited in all city residents and to the white with black skin (the official intellectuals). The northern part of the country (45% of the land) which is free, or under the control of the State, has now a very sad fate. It is cut in half. A portion (5% or only cities) is governed by the President and his Okou conardes women ministers and the other part consisting of all the villages or rural areas, traditional, is controlled by farmers (Africans, Africans Africans). Farmers occupy 40% of the country song that is declared "free zone or government." They have become the new rebels. They have blocked all roads and all the tracks that lead to their villages. Their "police," "police," "soldiers" or "militia" to them watching them very, very well and effectively and jealously guard night and day. With extreme rigor and vigilance. They put a cross on the cities. The white world. On its realities. On his manners. Its institutions. Its values. Rotten. Came from France. Of America. Of England. Of Germany. Of Spain. Portugal. Etc … The farmers said goodbye to Gongonpô (white world, gwa language of Côte d'Ivoire). Farewell to blofouêkro (white country, language Agni of the Ivory Coast). This means that there is no more movement between cities and villages Okoupô. The villagers have stopped feeding, maintaining the urban and obey them.

After three months of rebellion village, famine descends mercilessly on cities causing disease and death. People are hungry. They are hungry. Emaciated. Stunted. Sickly. Emaciated. Emaciated. As Ethiopian children. Because they are totally deprived of food supply. In cities, more bananas, cassava, yams, taro, chillies, potatoes, onions, okra, eggplant, tomatoes, palm seeds, fruits, fish, meat etc.., etc. … It's terrible. Pitiful. Surprising to see that the urban (or white with black skin) can not do anything. For food. Not to starve. Surprising to find that they are nothing without the peasants. Really surprising that they have followed them, their welfare and salvation to the villagers that they so despise. Surprising to see that the city is totally dependent of the village, the village is above the city, the village that is useful and even indispensable to the city.

Surprising to see that the village stands on its own, he lives without the city when the city can not live without the village. Surprisingly, the city is a slave and that the village is his master. But then the white with black skin are the masters and important people by the demagogic discourse, the words misleading, deceptive, for the European languages, colonial (French, English, Spanish, German, Portuguese) they speak or write. Oh! Therein lies their value. Their worth. All their greatness. Full force; Beyond, they can not exist.

I understand why they bless as European settlement, so fiercely defend imperialism, racism, colonialism and all its products and all its avatars as globalization, capitalism, liberal democracy, republic, centralized unitary state, nation state, law Man and Citizen. All these things they protect and maintain a strong home, Land of diamonds, give them opportunities unheard of too great privileges, monopolies and untold power. All their happiness comes from there. With these things (these tricks), for example, they are Presidents of the Republic, heads of state, ministers, deputies, mayors, directors, senators, ambassadors, prefects, deputy prefects, budget-officials (paid too much, ruineurs) prime ministers, employees, thieves, embezzlers of public funds, surfactureurs, bribers, racketeers, soldiers and wealthy warriors, bandits and killers free and happy, looters and destroyers unrepentant criminals and released offenders, prostitutes, homosexuals and legal.

Ah! These things are really interesting too! Too good to be condemned and abandoned by them. But they are definitely harmful to the villagers. They have all lost to the Republic of my ass. Cobi! Covan! Van! Van! (Con rotten! Con dirty! Sale! Sale!). They have all given a gift to the Republic of my ass. Their lives, their blood, their crops, their land, their fields, gold, diamonds, oil, iron, copper, uranium, etc.., Etc.., Etc.. Enough is enough. Too much dominance, too much contempt, flying too, too much alienation, too expropriation, dispossession too, too much abuse. That revolt. It grows in the war a. A bis rebellion. This is the fate of Okoupô gruesome and pitiful. Where everything is rotten. Where everyone is rotten. Perverted. Depraved. Corrupted. Unless the people of the new countries created by the new rebels, peasants. This new country new rebel bears a new name. The new name is Sramblékro. This means the land of blacks. The country of true blacks decolonized, independent, peaceful, happy, brave, courageous, honest and sincere. Sramblékro is the first and only country of true blacks in Africa, which are no longer Africans. Because Africa and Africans are creatures, slaves, puppets, robots and things of whites.

The Srambléens (Sramblékro residents) are revolutionary radicals, separatists irreducible. They want freedom and they conquered. They are now free and liberated from dictatorship (authoritarian, unjust), tyranny (arbitrary power, cruel, sanguinary), despotism (absolute power, arbitrary) of Okoupô. They have freed themselves from oppression, humiliation, bondage and domination infernal Okou, its "djandjous" of women ministers and their guardians, employers and accomplices white (Djandjou mean bitch, prostitutes in Ivorian slang).

This unique event, the most important of our century and this millennium is celebrated in grand style. Throughout Sramblékro. This is the popular rejoicing. Singing and dancing warriors in all villages, all fields and all the camps. In every family, every court, being celebrated this great victory over the demons, devils and the enemies of city dwellers, intellectuals and white rotten villains, bloodthirsty parasites, leeches, now condemned to die of hunger. Each farmer has found happiness, the joy of life, peace, dignity and prosperity is as proud as a rooster. Everyone is grateful to his pious and sincere personal genius, the genius of his village and all the gods who helped and supported the struggle for freedom, independence real and absolute. But special prayers and special thanks (prayers and thanks collective, formal national) are addressed to a very great God collective, official, national. This God is none other than Biongon. Biongon is the official national God and all of Sramblékro animists. According to legend and cosmogony official and national Biongon is the creator, the protector, the unifier, the peacemaker, the liberator and savior of blacks Sramblékro. It was he who gave wisdom, intelligence, fortitude and unwavering commitment to fighters Sramblékro.

Biongon is the source of life and happiness of Srambléens (Sramblékro inhabitants). He is the guarantor of health, safety, salvation, prosperity and fertility of the villagers. It is celebrated annually by all the villagers, through the holiday yams, generations and sacrifices or offerings at the foot of the great baobab mythical, mystical and mysterious standing majestically between the villages and Domolon Dabre in the young sub-Ogloipô prefecture, near Petit-Alépé, Côte d'Ivoire. For villagers, it's all honor and glory of Biongon. For in him we owe everything. For villagers biongoniste must, at all times, think Biongon. We must pay tribute and thanks due to His infinite goodness, of his infinite generosity, his unfailing love and its uncountable benefits for men and all creatures. While eating, we must think of him. Drinking, we must think of him. Everyone owes him libations and offerings. At any time. Constantly.

Normal. It is the duty of the son. Recognition. Love. The affection. Tenderness. On behalf of communion and solidarity that should exist between a father and son. For their mutual happiness.

Now, I talk about the national policy Sramblékro. Her name Paysanocratie. This is a new word. Is it not? A word that does not please revolutionary whites, official intellectuals, false Democrats and Republicans Okoupô false. This is the shit. This is the shit. This is crap. Shit shit. Shit squared for them. It is their nemesis. Their mortal beast. Paysanocratie. Ah! Ah! It's terrible that. This is terrible. What does that mean, right? Who created the word barbaric, ugly, violent and politically? It is an inhabitant of the new country. A resident of Sramblékro. This is Toissin.

In my profession, I question and I'm talking people interesting. People who are in politics. People who make peace. All those who make history. I watch everyone. I'm politicians everywhere. I am their friend and enemy. They flee from me. But I approach. I cling to them. Some confide in me. I am their spokesman indirect, informal. Their judge. Their spiritual director. I blame, criticize, denounce them or glorify them. I am very uncomfortable or very friendly. It depends…. Very annoying or fun for them by my writing or glowing lightning. I'm afraid, feared and hated. But also loved and pampered. This is according … Job requires. Is it not?

Any job has its risks, its drawbacks and its advantages. I have the privilege of meeting the most famous people, have dinner with them, interview them. I had dinner with Jacques Chirac, George Bush, Tony Blair, with Okou with Adowa. Ah! Ah! Ah! It's really nice. Nice to be with these great. Into their beautiful world of bourgeois too well fed, too corrupt and too rotten. But … it also runs the greatest risk. Yes, the greatest risk. We agree to be corrupt to be complicit and evil or laudatory, on the contrary, we choose to be murdered by them, to be their mortal enemy by refusing to support them and be their accomplice. But the golden rule of ethics or my job called Ethics says: "Without the freedom to criticize, no flattering praise." But politicians, gangsters of this world, do not want to hear that their ears criminal. Selfishness, megalomania (delusions of grandeur) and human evil force.

Resist these vices and virtues essential to the teaching of morality, law and religion. And the Burkinabe journalist independent (independent means incorruptible, insoumissible), Norbert Zongo was murdered, burned in his car, in Burkina Faso. Rest his soul! Gambian journalist Aïdara independent, was murdered in the Gambia. Rest his soul! The independent French journalist Jean Helene, was killed in Ivory Coast, rest his soul! The independent French-Canadian journalist Guy-André Kieffer, kidnapped in Côte d'Ivoire. He disappeared in Côte d'Ivoire. It was not found for years. Rest his soul! These unfortunate event of my colleagues murdered around the world are legion. Alas! Good God! Amonbin! (Your mother's cunt, gwa language of Côte d'Ivoire). Cobi! VANOC (con dirty! con rotten language of Côte d'Ivoire). Krobri! krovan (Country dirty! rotten country!). Shit shit!

Oh God Biongon! God of pure justice! God of justice and just right. God of pure freedom! God of freedom and free free! Will you tolerate all these violent crimes? Will you forgive these monsters, these vampires, these bandits and the bandits always bloodthirsty politicians who dare to take the life of their fellows, their compatriots, their subjects and to other humans? Will you forgive these ungodly, to the Unbelievers, who do you honor points and honor points that the world you have created so much suffering for love? Biongon Lord, Thou art the only Savior of all, your duty is it not correct and punish the evil that the world is more just, more beautiful and happier?

I am a war reporter without borders. That's also a very big risk. It is the supreme risk. I am loyalist fighters as rebel fighters in the war. I am everywhere. I shoot them all in action. I shoot the dead, corpses. I count them, I take stock of the fighting. I go to jail with prisoners of war. I attend the abuses and torture appalling. Many prisoners are daily executed, hanged, shot or slaughtered before my eyes curious. I may sometimes be confused or equated with prisoners of war. But still I managed to defend myself, to escape the violent death, suffering excruciating torture or to Calvary inflicted on real prisoners. My secret is to always promise the protagonists, the combatants on both sides (rebels and loyalists) to be neutral, impartial, in processing information, to be fair, honest (complacent and complicit) to them and never give false information. But to say only "truth nice." Do you know what it is? The "truth nice" is the truth that does not bother them. The truth that does not compromise the eyes of the world. In the eyes of the UN, the International Community. Got all that. Is it not?

The murderers, the killers and torturers of all stripes love to enjoy absolute impunity. As saints. Like angels. Like children at heart. Yep. They are big cheaters. So they abhor the denunciations of the free, independent and responsible. They like to hurt and harm in secret. They fear too grunts of the UN, EU, AU, ECOWAS, Human Right Watch, Amnesty International, all international organizations and Human Rights and Citizen. So you understand that a journalist (the international body called Lightning) like me, among them, represents a great danger. For them it is very worrying for them. They see me more as a spy. A clever spy to kill. As a clever spy to control very strictly and watch very, very closely. For their safety. For their happiness. Cobi! VANOC (con dirty! con rotten). Fucking hell! Shit shit! It is in these hellish conditions of death threats, harassment in all directions, suspicion, blackmail and endless suffering that I have done my job everywhere in Africa, America, Europe, Asia and Oceania. It's and I worked Okoupô has Sramblékro to gather facts and information I give you here in this book very rude and very dirty in places. This book is very dirty and very rude in places because it recounts the facts very coarse and very dirty in this world. Facts that happen every day in countries very coarse and very dirty. Yes, countries with very coarse and very dirty as Okoupô, Côte d'Ivoire, DRC, Congo, Angola, Algeria, Somalia, Sudan, Liberia, Sierra Leone etc.. deserve to be denounced, condemned, insulted and erased from the earth. With their leaders odious, shameful and unscrupulous scoundrels. So the things that happen there are odious, shameful and dirty! Amonbin! (Your mother's cunt!) Cobi! VANOC-van (con dirty! con rotten, totally rotten!).

We journalists, read a lot. We are bookworms. We have teachers and guides. They are very cultured people, highly educated: scholars, sages, philosophers, thinkers, humanists. Mine is Toissin. This is a very popular African philosopher. He is the father, the creator of the Afrocratisme and Paysanocratie two doctrines philosophical and political, which have inspired and guided the revolutionaries who founded Sramblékro. To decode and understand the current socio-political, I refer to him. It is the greatest theorist and specialist Okoupô. He has published two books highly critical of this strange country. It is not at all kind to the policies, politicians and politicos Okoupô. He sharply attacked, and denounce them violently condemned without appeal. I love her very objective reading of history okoupéenne, its analysis and its deep and picturesque description of situations and tragedies. On Sunday, August 20th… at 2:00 p.m., I held out my microphone friendly hyper sensitive to collect his last impressions of intellectual expert Okoupô. Here's what he told me just before his final departure from his country towards America:

"I, Toissin, I am a citizen and a native of Okoupô. But I find politics okoupéenne abominable, execrable and monstrous. This is evil and demonic. I have always fought by my pen. The result of my struggle is beautiful. It is the creation of Sramblékro. I'm very proud. My mission in Africa is over. Sramblékro save all the other parts of Africa. I am preparing to go rescue the Western countries that are ravaged by crises and endless wars. First, I aim America. Okoupô start from. This is the land of evil and everything is negative. A Okoupô, we saw several political regimes come and go. We went successively to "Baoulécratie" (bloodthirsty tyranny or dictatorship and socio-economically criminal Baule of Ivory Coast with the Presidents Felix Houphouet-Boigny and Aimé Bédié) to "Yacoubacratie" (tyranny or dictatorship and bloody socioeconomically criminal Yacouba of Ivory Coast President with General Robert Guei), the "Bétécratie" (bloodthirsty tyranny or dictatorship and socio-economically criminal Bete of Ivory Coast President Laurent Gbagbo with) and "Dioulacratie" (bloodthirsty tyranny or dictatorship and socio-economically criminal Dioula with Ivory Coast President Alassane Ouattara.

"Baoulécratie," "Yacoubacratie," "Bétécratie" and "Dioulacratie" are "criminocraties" of "malocraties" of "bêtisecraties" of "sauvagecraties" of "brigandocraties" of "banditocraties" and "mafiocraties." The "Bétécratie" says: "A thousand deaths left thousand dead right, I advance." Word of the Bete President Laurent Gbagbo of killings, massacres and atrocities committed by his countless bloody regime, draconian and bellicose. "I give ten years of civil war in Ivory Coast if I can hunt, says Laurent Gbagbo. We are well into barbarism integral ("Barbarocratie"), the full cynicism ("Cynocratie"), warmongering full ("Bellocratie"). All this is appalling and disgraceful to the civilized mind, disciplined, healthy and holy. This is intolerable and unacceptable for us. "No Gbagbo, Ivory Coast No," say supporters, militia, Liberian mercenaries of Gbagbo during the terrible civil war in Ivory Coast. They are looters, robbers, killers, murderers and unrepentant destructive. They want to destroy Ivory Coast (and they did it) and kill all its inhabitants if we remove Gbagbo from power. Trillion CFA francs were said to be, expended in the purchase of weapons to kill all anti-Gbagbo in Ivory Coast. In this logic, it is no longer any question of organizing presidential elections just, fair, transparent Gbagbo could lose. Proponents of the latter say, "We win or we win." This means, in clear: in all cases, the power is confiscated by any means.

Thus, although soundly beaten at the polls in the presidential election on November 28, 2010, Mr. Gbagbo did not want to cede power to Alassane Ouattara proclaimed winner and recognized by the world. He preferred to engage the world in the war in Ivory Coast on a hypothetical cash relief and divine miracle to win this global war unjust and retain power. His many sycophants, priests, pastors, imams, prophets, courtiers, religious, generously fed, maintained and corrupt to the bones (cost of billions) predicted his victory. They strongly supported and encouraged stupidly and selfishly hurt and make war unfair, unjustified and unjustifiable to Ivorians, Africans, Americans, Europeans and Asians who condemn Bétécratie (stupid, senseless, murderous, fatal suicidal) and Laurent Gbagbo. The "democracies" have destroyed the entire Ivorian Ivory Coast (by plunder, devastation, sabotage, theft, robbery) and killed off millions of men, women and innocent children. This is the effect of laws Okoupô: "You win or win," "A thousand deaths left thousand dead right, I start," "Gbagbo No, No Ivory Coast" (Eburnia is delenda) "I promise ten years of civil war in Ivory Coast in the event of my overthrow" etc.., etc.., etc.., "Bêtisecratie" squared. Disaster. Monstrosity. Plots, schemes, machinations, intrigues to infinity. Mafia. Flight. Lies. Demagoguery. Poor governance.

Mismanagement. Bad faith to infinity. Dishonesty to infinity. Ethnocracy. Intellectual, religious and criminal politicians squared.

Okoupéens the Ivory Coast are truly pitiful. Most of them are tortured. They died a violent death, atrocious, cruel and ugly. Death by firing squad, by torture, beating, hanging, starvation, by suffering, by burning (using tires, gasoline and matches) and machetes. Millions of people (men, women, children) innocent and defenseless and were killed, executed, murdered with impunity by young people and manipulated by fanatics camps Gbagbo and Ouattara throughout Côte d'Ivoire. The killing has become a game, a fun and trivial thing for child soldiers in war of political groups: LMP (Presidential Majority of Laurent Gbagbo) and RHDP (Rassemblement des Houphouetists for Democracy and Peace of Alassane Ouattara and Konan BEDIE).

Until the arrest of Laurent Gbagbo occurred Monday, April 11, 2011, by the military coalition grouping Republican Forces (FRCI) created by Alassane Ouattara, the Blue Helmets of the UN and the Soldiers of the French Operation Unicorn, Côte d'Ivoire was one vast cemetery and a hospice in Okoupô formidable and feared. Mass graves filled with human corpses and mass graves were visible everywhere: in fields, houses, villages, streets... The executioners put therein fire and rejoiced to see the bodies of their victims burn and explode. They filmed these shows proudly and joyously macabre and terrifying with their cell phones and then sold these films video cassette CD anywhere in the world, to make money.

"Eburnia delenda is" (Côte d'Ivoire must be destroyed or it will destroy the Ivory Coast, in Latin). This is the heritage as a poisoned chalice that is left to Alassane Ouattara, great economist. This task is to heal all the wounded, the sick and resurrect all the dead and to compensate them. Then he must rebuild the Ivory Coast, stabilize and revitalize its economy. He must develop a sustainable Côte d'Ivoire, quantitatively and especially qualitatively. It must abolish, remove the very famous Article 125 of the martial law Okoupô. (100 CFA francs CFA 25F gasoline and matches to kill a man by burning him alive.) This is what Article 125 youth and children killers. Act murderers and killers unscrupulous moral and spiritual Okoupô."

CHAPTER 6

I return to the national policy Sramblékro. I have not forgotten. I just wanted to tell you first things that touch me deeply. Things too dirty, too ugly to make me cry. This is what you read remember the speech of the philosopher Toissin. But the national policy of the new country (Sramblékro) is very different and very interesting for all true revolutionaries, real Democrats and real Republicans. That is why we must study it, analyze it well and expose it in full (in detail, length and width). This policy is, as we have seen, called the paysanocratie. This name was given to him by a gentleman named Owagnintin (or wise, or gwa M'Batto language of Côte d'Ivoire). The wise Owagnintin, aka Toissin, defines the neologism (new word) of the Government as paysanocratie farmers by farmers and for farmers.

This is democracy. True democracy. The only. The unique. The best in the world. And non-farmers by the government officials and intellectuals for intellectuals (the intellectocratie). The minority of intellectuals that are Okoupô government for itself, for itself, for its own interests unjust. The intellectocratie is unfair, undemocratic and unacceptable. The paysanocratie is the only truly democratic political system that fits absolutely perfectly and the Blacks, Africans and peasants. This is the only legitimate and effective political system. Paysanocratie means Liberation, Revolution and Renaissance. This system is made Sramblékro on these three principles (SCRA). While fools Okopéens vegetate, languish and eke shame, unfortunately, cowardly and foolishly in intellectocratie (disguised as democracy), colonization and imperialism Franco-Western (the occidentalocentrisme), the Srambléens (or Sramblékras) have resettled by the Revolutionary War just in their own customs and their own political traditions. They have reclaimed their cultures and civilizations. Courageously. Heroically. Without fear. No inferiority complex. Without complex non-white or unbleached. Without complex non-westernized. And time of globalization and westernization of Africa accelerated. Contempt and to detriment of the West. To the chagrin of France-Africa and La Francophonie. What bravery! What audacity! What bravery! What a challenge! What slaps the white devils and demons!

Sramblékras how could they do that? Saying an emphatic and definitive to the Republic, to the unitary nation state, democracy fictitious white, imperialism, racism, colonialism and cultural discrimination, spiritual, intellectual and civilization to which they were subjected before. The price of their blood. By giving their heads cut whites and intellectuals official Okoupô. But how? What they did really and concretely? How did they build their country? Clearly, what fundamental difference there between Sramblékro and Okoupô? Well, it's simple. Unlike Okoupô, Sramblékro has no President of the Republic. But a king over kings. A supreme king. Democratically elected by his peers-kings, by lot. Its mandate is five years. Non-renewable. Another king should succeed him. By lot and also for a period of five years. Also non-renewable term. And so on. At infinity. It is a rotating system which will see the kings or chiefs govern both their own kingdoms and ethnic communities and the great new Community (composed of all ethnic groups who have withdrawn from the Republic intellectocratique and the nation state, order to govern themselves according to their own wisdom, by their own African customs and their own laws to govern their own affairs. With honesty and efficiency. In any freely and brotherhood. Without murderous rivalry with other ethnic groups. without war. Without violence of any kind. Without armed rebellion. Without coup. Without tribalism. Without disorder. Without barbarism. Without cynicism. In this new system, each ethnic group is independent, autonomous and sovereign. On all plans. It is free and may maintain relations of any kind with whom she wants. According to his own wisdom and culture.

At its best interests. Sramblékro is a kind of confederation of legitimate and consensual mile races spread over the entire territory. These ethnic groups are now operating freely and responsibly for their own happiness, their own soil and their own basement fabulously rich. They have no accountability to whites. They have to report only to them themselves. They are responsible only to themselves. King Supreme, Nanan, is controlled and assisted in its formidable task by all the other kings. They can blame him, punish him or remove him in case of gross negligence, of treason or serious breach of duty on his part. Thus Sramblékro is very well governed, well managed and very well managed. For blacks and villagers themselves. For them alone. behalf of their ancestors. From their traditions millennia and their great God Biongon. Security is complete. Peace is total. health is perfect. Happiness is total. Food safety is total. Prosperity is total. Freedom is total. justice is total. Democracy is total. Who said that Negroes, blacks, farmers, bushmen, the" wild" do not know how to govern? Democratically? a republican? Legally? Rationally? whites and modernist black intellectuals, and intellectocrates occidentalocentristes (those who view the West as the center of the world as the best part of the world as the top), you lie too much on account of African farmers. You are ignorant, ignorant, ignorantissimes. You are also in bad faith. Too bad faith. You despise the peasants wrongly. You infantilisez in the wrong. Your glance appraiser is reversed. You are sick. You are schizophrenics (those who do not see the face it). You take their infinite happiness to misery and endless woe you take your infinite for infinite happiness. You take their reason and unreason unreason deadly to your right. You take their infinite wisdom and infinite follies follies your infinite wisdom to infinite. You take their splendid civilization to barbarism disgraceful and shameful barbarism for your splendid civilization. You take their incomparable religion-animism and witchcraft-sorcery animism your ideal religion. You take their science knowledge and childish ignorance perfect for your childish ignorance for science-perfect knowledge. Etc., etc.., etc.. This is sad. Too sad. Mercy and pity for you. Fuck the shit! Toivan! (penis dirty! Penis rotten!). In language Baule of Cote Ivory.

Trapped, suffocated, crushed and degraded by the autocratic policy (based on the dictatorship and tyranny), mythocratique (based on lies), kleptocratic (based on theft, embezzlement, looting and chaos) and malocratique (based on evil), the Okoupéens flee en masse to Europe and America. To escape death, famine, unemployment, misery, poverty, disease. They migrate. Go into exile. Be deported. In the countries most affected and most dangerous in the world (the affected countries are those who suffer from ailments such attacks, hurricanes, terrorism, rebellion, cold, earthquake, unemployment, illness…): France, England, Italy, Germany, USA, Canada, Spain, Portugal, Belgium. They use all means to leave Okoupô. They go through the Maghreb countries: Morocco, Tunisia, Algeria, Libya, Mauritania. Most of them end their adventure in the Spanish enclaves of Séouta and Méliya. There, they break your nose against the son of fences and barbed wire which separate Spain from Morocco. They are sandwiched by the military, the police and the Moroccan police and their Spanish counterparts. Who mind the day and night patrolling in the forests and along their common borders.

No pity for the undocumented. They are tortured, humiliated, massacred and killed. Mercilessly for undocumented migrants. They are sometimes thrown into the sea To the delight of sharks and whales and hungry raptors. Nightmare. Infernal paradise. Mirage. Illusion. This is still not enough to deter millions of adventurers or would-be emigrants. Yes, it's a macabre consequences of political self-mythologies-kleptocratic Okoupô of whose capital is called paradoxical paradise. What biting irony! What sarcasm!

The massive illegal immigration of Africans to the West is generally an act of desperation. It is a cry of distress. Of pain. This is the open expression of a ras-le-bol and failures African socio-political. This is one of the dramatic consequences of the barbaric policy, cynical and belligerent African leaders. This is the result of the "barbaro-cyno-bellocratie" on a continent that is full of riches yet of any kind. The richest continent in the world. Yes, it must be said bluntly. No offense to the imperialists, racists Manichaeans, to Western neo-colonialists and their lackeys in Africa. Crazy, crazy, crazy squared. Thugs, hoodlums and thugs squared. Bandits and bandits squared. Robbers, thieves and robbers to the square. Murderers, assassins and murderers squared. Rot squared. Squared ugliness. Evil squared. Selfishness squared …

In Paris, London, Bertin, New York, Madrid, Lisbon etc.., Black immigrants, Africans, are hunted down, brutalized and humiliated by police officers. Treated undocumented and demons, they are chained and thrown like slaves in airplanes to Abidjan, Bamako, Dakar, Conakry, Libreville, Douala, Kinshassa, Ouagadougou, Lagos etc.. They are modern slaves. Without dignity. Without rights. Without freedom. Their crime? They went begging. They went begging. They covet the "cake" and "happiness" of whites. They entered the Christian Paradis, paperless. Without authority of Jesus Christ. Where they are repressed, deported and sent back to hell. Like the damned. They have no place in Christian Paradise. Paperless, these wretched of the earth are not men. They are animals or things awkward, bulky and need to remove harmful, destroy. To be free, at peace, happy, rich, safe. But the deuce! Why white people are they from Africa? Why are they came to colonize Africans, looting and stealing all their wealth and their possessions? Why are they so ungrateful towards Africans whom they used to develop their countries and build their paradise? Why, why and why? Shit shit! Toibi! Toivan! (Penis dirty! Penis rotten! Language Baule of Côte d'Ivoire).

In the Philosophy Toissin, I went to meet his Majesty Nanan, King Supreme Sramblékro. A new country. A country of blacks. Created by blacks. And for blacks. Only for blacks. I handed him my microphone provocative. To get his feelings on Okoupô, Sramblékro enemy countries. He graciously answered all my questions. Straightforward.

Your Majesty, hello! Can you tell me why you decided to leave the Democratic Republic of Okoupô to create a new country, your country to you, which is totally opposed to the model of society and state that white colonizers have imposed on all Africans and the whole earth as the only path that can save humanity, like all the best and paradise for the world? What do you think of Okoupô? You left modernity and civilization to join the tradition, barbarism and savagery. Is this reasonable, interesting, useful, necessary for you and your people? Do you really have done so well? Are you happy now and save without the whites? Do not you fear that your people may one day want to go back to live in the white world and assert white values which still exercise, I believe, a power of fascination for people of your country? Do you still able to successfully resist Western imperialism, without succumbing to its attacks, to come? Are you really ready to take forever to white head of this world that you challenge and, with such arrogance? If yes, what are your means? What do you expect to win all the battles to come and win victory over your enemies? Do not you fear that the imperialist West come one day, by all means, you impose the worship of his five favorite (or Trojans) of democracy, respect for human rights, the Republic, globalization and modernity, as it does around the world? What do you think of Iraq, Afghanistan, Yugoslavia, Zimbabwe, North Korea, Côte d'Ivoire, Libya? I invite you to think about the fate of leaders like: Saddam Hussein, the Molar Omar, Slobodan Milosevic, Robert Mugabe, Thomas Sankara, Patrice Lumumba, Marien N'Gouabi, Camara, Sekou Toure, Kwame Nkrumah, Muammar Gaddafi. Do not you fear for your life and the lives of your people? Want to become a martyr like them? I'm done, I'm listening.

Thank you, Mr. Journalist, Mr. everybody's friend and person. For this is your nickname here. And you deserve to great effect. Thank you for your interest in my country, Sramblékro, my creature. And thank you for the opportunity you gave me to share my thoughts, my actions and my country to the world through your large and prestigious international journal called, rightly, the Lightning.

I tell you that here in Sramblékro, people love to read your journal and especially your articles because they are very well written, because they are very objective. Very true. Very interesting. And very bold. You are very brave. I ask you to continue on this path. It is safe. Now, please faithfully my answers to your many questions relevant and provocative. My colleagues and I decided kings to leave Okoupô because it is by no Democratic or Republican. And like us, we want real democracy and genuine republic, and condemn the sham, the illusion and hypocrisy, we have created ourselves.

We believe that the only way that can save humanity is the political model of Sramblékro. The paysanocratie. This is what there is best for the world. Sramblékro is heaven on earth. Other peoples of the earth, looking too happy, well-being and salvation we must imitate. They must take their lead from us. They must create their paysanocratie them. Okoupô is a very bad model. This model is a catastrophic policy. It's the plague and gangrene that whites gave to the whole world through their expansionism.

Okoupô is the main theater or the capital of evil. Vice. Of all the devilry that enrich the whites. At the expense of life. This is the No. 1 theater of living dangerously: war, rebellion, coups, anarchy, barbarism, savagery, delinquency, crime, banditry etc..

Women in this country are all naked in the streets. Sacrilege! They love the outdoors, in nature, in public, everywhere. Without embarrassment. With men and with women. O sacrilegious! Men make love with men. How horrible! Men and women make love to animals, dead, through the anus, mouth, ears, nostrils etc.. How horrible! What sacrilege! Men have children with men, marry legally with men and the Christian church. O sin! The women have children with women, married women and lawfully with the Christian church. O sin!

The people of this country are lawless. They are sharks. They kill and devour each other. This is anarchy. The jungle. A can of worms. Anything goes in this hell. Nothing is forbidden. In this hell, everything is sold and everything is achieved by money alone. A Okoupô, everyone is an enemy of everyone. This is the war of all against all. On behalf of the interest. On behalf of the money that is the supreme value. The real god. Living. Concrete. Money is the only god worshiped and listened to Okoupô. Everything, absolutely everything, is done in its name. Everything, absolutely everything, is done by him and for him. Okoupô is a crazy world, patients. It is the world of misery, anguish, sadness, violence, widespread insecurity, death. A Okoupô, men drink pee and eat the excrement of their wives. We do not want them here. There everyone wants to be President of the Republic, Head of State, Prime Minister, Minister, MP, Mayor, Director, Warden, and official ambassador. Molest children their parents every day and students and students chicotent and mortally wound their teachers every day. With impunity. There is no discipline. They close the school and go on leave as they please. They are kings. They are above the government and the President of the Republic. They kill, hang, burn their comrades with impunity. All halls are held hostage by them. They sell or rent all the rooms to civilians. They raise taxes on any trade that takes place on campus. They extort money from everyone on campus.

We do not want such things to us. There, the rebels, militia private, military, gendarmes, police and mercenaries are confused. They clash. They kill, steal, kill, rape women, men and children. It's chaos. The imbroglio. The shambles. That's why we got out of there. Today, we are free. Flourished. Happy. Saved. We are very, very well in our country to us. And no foreigner can we persuade or convince us otherwise.

Here, no foreigner has the right or authority to dictate our course of action, our politics, our ideas, our feelings and actions. No foreigner knows the nature of our happiness. No foreigner can not appreciate the things and values for us. No foreigner should judge us. No foreigner should enjoy anything for us. We are free, independent and sovereign. We are the first and the only ones like that around the world. And we're very, very proud. We hope very much that all the peoples of Africa and elsewhere as we are. We will fight for their liberation, their independence and happiness. In solidarity. Our altruistic morality requires us to. A Okoupô is the intellectocratie, that is to say, the tyranny of official intellectuals, westernized minority, against the peasant majority (99% of the population). We do not want it. There is the occidentalocentrisme, that is to say, the complete and absolute domination of Africans by the West, that is to say the total hegemony (or the absolute triumph) of the race white on the black race and its culture. We do not want it. On behalf of seven core values, sacred Liberty, Independence, Sovereignty, Dignity, Justice, Peace, Happiness. A Okoupô is the prevailing materialism, that is to say the murderous competition for material wealth, the rat race and fatal to the acquisition of the overabundance of wealth in real socio- material. There is modernity and civilization and white pervertissantes dépravantes: industrialization dangerous, atheism, political secularism, destruction of the ozone layer, air pollution, water, atmosphere, warming the land, climate disruption, cataclysms, individualism, selfishness, toxic waste, diseases, deaths, etc.. We do not want any of that. We prefer the quiet life, traditional, spiritualized, moral, natural, healthy, pure. Our unique model is the NATURE. And we follow his laws. An unshakeable. Rigorous. This is the source of our health, our security, our peace, our happiness and our salvation. We love NATURE and BIONGON.

Confucius, a Chinese sage, called on men to live according to TRADITION (the values of the past). He's right. Lao Tzu, another Chinese sage, called on men to live by the law of NATURE (this is called Taoism). He too is right. The paysanocratie is everything. If you want to turn this into a universal school of thought, in a SCHOOL, in an education in an ideology or a philosophy for Africans call it the Afrocratisme. A new word. Is it not? Put that in all minds, in all the dictionaries and encyclopedias in all. This is good for White, Yellow for, for the Reds and Blacks. Explain it to everyone. Spread this everywhere. It can save the whole world and all humanity. It is a liberating thought, and generating revolutionary virtues. We educate all our fellow men, women, young and old, in Afrocratisme. This conditions them and makes them absolutely very fervent patriots and nationalists. So no one would dream of Sramblékra Okoupô to leave. Never, ever and ever. I bet my head for that. No outsider can never impose on us its models and its values. None of this can no longer walk with us in Sramblékro. We are now incolonisables.

Western imperialism in all its forms, has definitely failed here at home. It failed to face our great determination. Given our deep conviction. Facing our absolute firmness. Facing our bravery. Facing our heroism. Our main weapon of struggle is our unshakable faith. We have faith in ourselves. We have faith in our revolutionary action. We have faith in our ideal paysanocratique. Our strength and support key is the Afrocratisme. We rely only on ourselves. Our courage. Our revolutionary will. And that is enough.

The coalition racist, imperialist and western terrorist could occupy Iraq, Afghanistan and Libya because there is no paysanocrate (supporter of paysanocratie) nor Afrocrate (supporter, follower of Afrocratisme) in these countries. Thus these countries are weak and vulnerable. Occupiable. Vincibles. And the inhabitants of these Arab countries became corrupted, dominate, divide, manipulate and stupidly tame by whites. There have been selfish, traitors and cowards among them. Patriotism, nationalism, citizenship and loyalty have been sorely lacking in these countries. Too bad for them. This is not the case at all of Sramblékro. I have said enough of the qualities and virtues of my country, Sramblékro. I think that leaders like Saddam Hussein, Milosevic, Thomas Sankara, Patrice Lumumba, Qaddafi Mohamar, Marien Ngouabi, Sekou Toure, Robert Mugabe, Kwame Nkrumah and others do not have the luck and wisdom we have. They have not applied the paysanocratie and Afrocratisme. They unfortunately do not know these two things which are our main assets and instruments of combat. Among those leaders who are still living and who are still in power, gain to follow our example, to read and study the Afrocratisme. It is absolutely necessary for them. It's good for their success and salvation. Finally, let me say that I did not at all afraid. Or for my personal life or the life of my people. I am a fighter. My people are a fighting people. And a fighter should not be afraid of his enemy. The victory is ours. Forever. Vive Sramblékro! Down with imperialism! Biongon Sramblékro protect and bless! Thank you."

Okoupô goes wrong. Very badly. He lives still hot hours. Hot days. Weeks of very warm. Warmer months. All the talks failed. All negotiations have failed. All peace agreements and cease-fire, national reconciliation and reunification of the country have failed. None of that is respected by the belligerents and the protagonists of the crisis perennial (endless). The thousand UN resolutions to bring peace and order in the country are not applied. As in Côte d'Ivoire, DRC, Somalia, Liberia, Sierra Leone etc.. The Okoupéens blithely flout with impunity and the UN, ECOWAS, the AU, the EU…. Well, the international community has no authority and no efficacy Okoupô. She is totally helpless. Its representatives are intimidated, threatened, killed. All vehicles marked A (United Nations) who wanders the streets of Paradise is ransacked or burned. The national reconciliation government comprising rebels, opponents and supporters of Okou failed. He has not worked. The transitional government has failed. He has not worked.

The national constitution has lapsed. It can no longer apply. It does more than organize the general elections (presidential, municipal, legislative) and govern the country. She is fiercely contested by the rebels and opponents. It is considered anti-democratic, anti-republican, bellogène, partisan, xenophobic and discriminatory tribalique. Indeed, by some of its provisions, it prevents some individuals having the nationality okoupéenne. She refuses nationality or citizenship to certain people from the opposition who have tried before. Suddenly, they no longer qualify as candidates for the presidential election. For section 100 of this constitution clearly states: "Can not be a candidate for President of the Republic that the citizen who was born and has always stayed in the country after national independence, with his mother and father them themselves born in the country after national independence, and belonging to ethnic and caste Otonbou founder Okoupô."

The legal citizen of Okouopô is, indeed, one that is well described by this article discriminatory constitutional, frustrating and belligerent (which breeds war). Are therefore excluded from citizenship, entitling the eligibility and présidentiabilité, members of other ethnic groups, all foreigners naturalized okoupéens well as the many descendants of immigrants from Burkina Faso, Mali, Guinea, Senegal, Togo, Benin, French, Lebanese, Ghanaian, Liberian, American, Chinese, Japanese, Korean etc. who built, for their efforts, their intelligence and their work, the Nation okoupéenne. With native or indigenous.

This caused a deep rift in relations between the inhabitants of Okoupô. There, on one side and citizens on the other hand, non-citizens or "aliens" are desperate to, too, citizens. Residents are frustrated and wronged in their rights. They allege a conspiracy, injustice, arbitrariness, xenophobia, extreme nationalism, ethnic cleansing, selfishness, theft, expropriation, ingratitude, malice and hatred of the part-Aboriginal citizens (Otonbou). It follows the civil war. The war between "real Okoupéens" and "false Okoupéens." Between "good citizens" and "bad citizens." This war can only end if 'outsiders' and those who are assimilated to them because of their surnames, their dialects, their mode of dress, their food, their religion, their culture and their civilization, obtain citizenship, citizenship and the right to stand candidates in the presidential election. And, most importantly, a chance to win this presidential election. The war will never end if their candidate became President of the Republic of Okoupô. This will have the advantage of allowing "foreigners" and similar to live well and better. To be more free. Happier. Richer. More worthy. Saved. In peace. Safe etc.. This is the cause and meaning of the internal armed rebellion and civil war in Okoupô. This greatly facilitates internal Western imperialism. And imperialists to exploit the full. The whole world benefits. To blackmail the President Okou. For the knees. To weaken and humiliate him up. Western imperialism benefits. Okoupô to ruin. To put it into decline. Okoupô anxiously awaiting the end of the shambles. Will she or will she not? The great seer of Paradise, named Djigbotiki, predicted a great misfortune for Okoupô. "What a pity more for a country that is already bruised and battered, who has already experienced all sorts of misfortune and tragedy? God, Allah, NIAMIEN (God Agni language of Côte d'Ivoire), Lago (God Bete language of Côte d'Ivoire), Yékin (God-language Gwa Ivory Coast) do they not pity poor and unfortunate? Are they not Love, Wisdom and Goodness? "Ask the skeptics, unbelievers or ungodly, watery eyes. The Christian God said the wages of the sinner is death. And everyone knows that Okoupéens are the biggest sinners of the earth. So they are expecting their divine punishment. But this punishment announced she will take what form? Fall when she? These are now the biggest concerns of bandits and criminals of all kinds of Okoupô. Churches, mosques and temples in all cities of Okoupô always full. The crystalline sounds of bells are heard everywhere. Each day. Any time. At any minute. At any second. People sing. Dance. Pray. Cry. Lament. In all the holy places. To ward off misfortune foretold. But will this be enough to move it, to commiserate and to calm the angry gods who consider Okoupéens like demons, the wicked, the hypocrites and inveterate pranksters to be destroyed?

In this feverish atmosphere and tense, the President and Prime Minister Okou Adowa organize a great forum called national reconciliation. It is under the auspices of ECOWAS, AU, EU and

UN. This forum brings together a... Wednesday, March 20, at the Presidential Palace, the Opponents, rebels, militias, mercenaries, NGOs, religious, foreign diplomats, members of government and all institutions, the military and police, all elected officials and all senior government executives. It was exactly noon. President Charles Okou pronounces the solemn speech opening the forum. A bomb of extraordinary power and monstrous explodes. In the very large and luxurious room of national holidays. At the Presidential Palace. And that's the end of everyone. Apocalypse Now Redux. Ah, barbaro-cyno-bellocratie, when you hold us! By the reign of barbarism, cynicism and war. It is the will of God and men of Okoupô. This is not the will of God who reigns over Biongon Sramblékro.

Okoupô population was in turmoil. The panic reached everyone. It was the total rout, the stampede for himself. Toissin but could not accept that. This was contrary to his moral biongoniste. He managed to bring the dead to life. He saved everyone. He asked his beloved Biongon for seven (07) clock hours. Naked. At the foot of a large cheese which he plucked several sacred sacred leaves. He crushed the sacred leaves in his hands until a holy sacred liquid. Then he put a drop of that sacred liquid into the eyes of each death muttering of sacred words. After one hour, all the dead miraculously awoke together. They found their minds and perfect health by the infinite generosity, the infinite love and infinite goodness of Biongon.

SECOND PART

CHAPTER 7

In the aftermath of the Apocalypse occurred Okoupô, Toissin, best of all of Biongon son, miraculously found himself in the West, the country of Uncle Sam borrowed Without any means of transport used by men until day. He arrived in America without using either plane or boat or train, or automobile, or swimming, or walking. He used only the divine power of Biongon in him. Toissin was in favor of this benevolent God. And it was not his first time to travel and or using this mysterious and sacred way for glorious. Every time he sought the help of Biongon, he obtained immediately and infallibly. He was on very intimate and very privileged with the greatest of God Sramblékro.

As great magician, Toissin, the African philosopher, who inspired and guided the revolution Sramblékro founder, was welcome in the country of Barack Obama. He took charge of Boston. Descendu the Greyhound bus, around 19heures GMT, from New York City, he was welcomed by Richie fraternally. This was posted at the station waving in the air a sign that it was written: "ICCP Wellcomes Toissin" (ICCP welcome Toissin). Richie was one of the bosses of ICCP (International Camp Counseling Program), American Institution who received youth and students around the world wishing to visit the land of Uncle Sam and volunteer work in the camps of holiday camps. These were known as Camp Counselors International (CCI).

Toissin had just obtained his doctorate in the humanities, philosophy section in his country. He wanted to work as a Counselor. His camp was located in the Roxbury neighborhood called, at Martin Luther King Boulevard. It was not far from Franklin Park and Washington Park, two beautiful parks with large number of materials for children and adults. He was comfortably accommodated in the hotel YMCA (Young Man's Christian Association or Association of Christian Youth) at Huntington Avenue, not far from Christian Science Center (Christed Academy of Sciences) and Prudential Center Tower, the tallest tower or the highest skyscraper in Boston. Life was good at the hotel. Toissin was upstairs. He played with the twelve American television channels, each specialized in a particular activity: theater, music, sports, culture, etc.. His room was well air conditioned. There were two chairs, a table, two chairs and a Bible. Toissin thoroughly read the Bible, studying the psalms while living in Krishna consciousness. He was a yogi, a great practitioner of yoga, an avid reader Hindu holy books such as Vedas, Bhagavad-Gita, the Mahabharata and the Upanishads. He meditated much. He did it several times a day. The morning he left his room to have breakfast at the hotel restaurant on the ground floor. There he discovered the infinite variety of American meals. He learned to eat hamburgers, cheeseburgers, hot dogs, scrambled egg, Kentucky fried chicken, drinking pasteurized milk, tini (fruit juices, dyes). After that he went to his day camp (day camp) in Roxbury.

The founder of Sramblékro spent all day in this camp where the wealthy American families filed their children the next morning to resume night. Toissin work was to mentor and educate these children in many middle-class entertainment, sporting and intellectual Counselors with other local and international. There was the program: games, entertainment, walks, excursions, visits to places symbolic, glorious history and culture. Toissin discovered and libraries, museums, cultural centers, aquariums, gardens, zoos and famous enterprises.

Usually Toissin borrowed a subway to get to work. But one day, he started late. He woke up at 7:00. To try to catch up, he had to stop a taxi, a Chevrolet big. His driver was an elderly black. Toissin sat in the taxi and the driver gave precise information about their destination and the way forward. It started with a bang. But instead of going straight to the goal indicated by Toissin, he took another direction, wrong direction. Later on complaints and lamentations of his worried passenger, who felt in danger, he pretended to ignore the shortcut path. He then turned and began thus far too much time to find the true path.

He finally arrived at Martin Luther King Boulevard. But to the chagrin of Toissin. The taxi meter was merciless to Africans: $ 45. Such was the amount that the Negro had to pay the Ivorian American Negro. But the Ivorian was not 45 dollars on him that morning. It was everything and everything in his hands $ 25. He handed it to the driver begging him to take it first and let it get the balance in his camp nearby. The taxi had stopped at the entrance of the camp. Such was the mortal sin committed the Ivorian that morning in Boston. The old driver pulled out his gun. A sophisticated pistol. He pointed it at face Toissin. He shook his whole being. He was enraged. "We do not do that in America. We do not do that in America. It costs the death. I'll kill you here this morning and I will never be anything. I'll blow your skull dirty negro! You are not fair and bold. I'll shoot," he said. And poom! Boom! Boom! Three pistol shots were fired. Toissin miraculously dodged all the bullets would have been like any good African, white magic insider who would be in danger. Three shots were heard again. Panic and outrage at the camp. Everyone came out to witness the unfolding drama. An African negro face an American negro. An extraordinary duel.

Toissin flew into a position of practicing Yoga Kungfu Taichi. This made him insensible, invulnerable, invincible and very concentrated. Soon the police arrived on the scene and fired five shots into the air. This dispersed the crowd curious and troublesome. Toissin screamed fierce that shook the entire neighborhood. Following the" magic" kiai exceptionally terrifying and never heard the taxi caught fire in full view of police stunned and helpless. The appeal was made to firefighters. But not before they arrived on the scene, the driver and his car were completely charred.

After this incident pathetic and unusual Toissin peacefully led his life in Boston. It was still shuttling between hotel and YAMCA camp. In the hotel, he met a white man of about fifty, whose name Jimy. He was known to all as a mathematics teacher. Jimy showed himself very friendly, generous and helpful to Toissin to infinity. Sometimes he invited the Ivorian to the restaurant, at its expense. He also invited into his room to listen to music, talk and follow certain television programs together. He regularly attended Toissin. He proposed to give free math courses. It was kind of exaggerated. Generosity exaggerated. Exaggeration of altruism. America. "But then there are people very good and divine in America! Everybody is not like the taxi driver who wanted to kill me! "Thought the Ivorian, remembering his past drama, his first time in America hot (hot time). "But then there are Americans humans, altruistic and selfless, who can even do charity and volunteer! "Never ceased to wonder about the attitudes Toissin Professor Jimy. "Jimy should certainly be an exception among the Americans I know and the opposite of brainless drunk driver who tried to kill me," he said. But one evening, Jimy Toissin came to his room. Against all odds, he began to stroke it. He grabbed firmly Toissin, threw him into the bed, lay down on him and tried to kiss her on the mouth. Toissin vigorously resisted him. Jimy insisted and persevered. He said he wanted to be her husband legitimate and legal. "Jimy, so you're a homo, a PD," asked Toissin flabbergasted. "Yes, of course I am. Everyone is like that here. This is very good, it is our custom. Each man was her husband or wife- man-man and every woman has a husband-wife or wife-woman. It is right and proper. God made it that way," pleaded proudly Jimy. "You say that homosexuality is your national custom. If true, it can only be right and proper in your eyes. It makes sense. Each of us is a socio-cultural product. Each is the product of his culture. Know that I am not in your culture. I'm not a Yankee. I am a stranger to your culture. I am a stranger to your custom. You had better live your American custom with an American like you. This one will understand you and accept you. But I belong to another culture. I belong to the African culture, Ivory Coast, Gwa (Gwa are the one in Akan ethnic group). My culture condemns homosexuality. At home, in Gwa countries, homosexuality is considered an abomination. It is a crime against humanity, against nature, a mortal sin. For Gwa, God did not create men to behave sexually in this way. Pederasty, pedophilia, lesbianism is not in my culture. To me, these are the horrors, anti-values. You can not know, now, how you became ugly, horrible, horrible to my eyes Gwabi of Domolon (Gwa young native village Domolon). Jimy, you got me disappointed. Now, I hate you, I loathe. You are a perverse and depraved dangerous for me. Do not try to infect me with your culture abominable to me pervert and deprave me. I fear you.

With us the Gwa, every man has his wife who is a real woman, natural and normal. And every woman has a husband who is a real natural and normal. Stops to caress me and tempt me with your vices calamitous. Get out of my room. Fast!, Retorted violently Toissin, unwilling to be outdone in this sparring match. He was keen to win this battle of values, the battle axiological and ethical, to speak the language of philosophers. Battle between a mathematician, a philosopher- moralist-humanist. Battle between two companies, society and Gwa or African American or Western society. "Accept, runs up, it's an order, requirement, an injunction, commandment, an obligation. You do not refuse it. You are currently in America. You're not in Africa, in your native bush. Be reasonable. Become normal. Let yourself get out of your civilization and savagery. You accept, you let me do that to you, you sodomize here now or I'll kill you. I'm seriously. I am very, very excited. You annoy me. You're a fool, idiot. You dare deny my love for you God! You refuse true love, pure love, natural, normal, legitimate, legal, perfect! You are truly African, Ivory Coast, Gwa, so savage, ignorant. I'll kill you for your idiocy, for your contempt and your hatred for American values and sacred to all America. You are insulting, arrogant, insolent and aggressive. America, by my hands, will you correct, you civilize, you cultivate, you settle down, Americanize you and educate you.

I repeat, you must let them. You give me your body, I really like, you give me your ass, which is perhaps very clean, or I'll kill you right away. Here is my gun. It is loaded. I'm not kidding. It will blow your head african wild." These words violent, barbaric and obscene were followed by punches and kicks. A fierce battle ensued between the two men who broke everything in the room. Toissin struggled with all his physical and mystical to control his attacker and snatched his revolver. Repeated shots were heard. Their loud noises and terrifying arrived at the restaurant. And within minutes, all staff and guests flocked to the door of Toissin. This door was broken and the crowd discovered in the room in a trance with Toissin Jimy reduced to impotence and nothingness. It was bathed in a pool of blood which gave a dizzying panic sensitive to weapons.

CHAPTER 8

The tragic event of the hotel Toissin forced to leave Huntington Avenue to go live in the district Dorchester. The Carter family welcomed him in her womb with open arms. This family consisted of a 80-year-old mulatto and an old black woman of 71. It was a couple materially rich but no child, who lived his life peacefully. She was happy to receive a young African cultivated, to console a bit, somehow, sterility and infertility of his, to combat his loneliness and satisfy his curiosity about Africa and Africans. She spoiled Toissin who, having twice escaped death, was now a dark thought about America and Americans it was just a repair things.

When he wakes up every morning and usually at six, his breakfast was ready. A breakfast consisting of bread, butter, eggs, jam, pasteurized milk, pickles, salad, fruit juices, cheeses and cakes. This is a paradise to forget Toissin, his two crosses or hell past. The Carters had a very luxurious villa of six spacious and attractive rooms. Toissin floating in one of these rooms decorated with beautiful paintings of Picasso and family photos beautiful, decorated chairs, color TV, telephone, a Bible and a Koran being housed in this place. Toissin listened to the music of jazz and blues coming out of the radio which was incorporated into his bed. It was crazy, he was a guitarist playing jazz and blues from Africa where he was nicknamed why BBKing. A glorious nickname recalling the famous American Bluesman. He was trying to support and interpret with his acoustic guitar tunes he listened to great jazz on the radio. He paid tribute to his masters American artists: BB King, Freddy King, Albert King, T. Bone Waker, Mady Water, Jimy Hendrix, Champion Jack Dupry, Jimi Smith, George Benson, Ray Charles, Buddy Guy ...

After his very hearty breakfast, he was escorted to his camp by his guardian Carter aboard a Mercury Cougar big shiny and brand new. In the evening after work, he returned home aboard the same car a hundred meters long and twenty meters wide, with a kitchen, a lounge, swimming pool and a room toilet in the living Carter was really sweet and fantastic. Toissin had never before experienced such a life, even in dreams. But one Sunday evening while on a picnic in Washington Park, Toissin was caught by a telephone call that told him the gruesome tragic death of Carter torque. A new shocking and appalling. The old couple who had just returned from a walk in Cambridge, died in a traffic accident. His Cougar Mercury fell into the Charles River, in the middle of the bridge, having slipped and violently struck the parapet. Was it the end of pure happiness and pure love, true, that Toissin endless and eternal hope! One Friday morning, denying the very fate of his tender famile host Toissin went to a geniculate pitifully along the Charles River. He was naked. Full of grief, he stared silently rushing waters of Charles and cruel. Eyes heavy with the tears, he began to pray to the God Biongon. This was her supernatural protector. It was he who led mysteriously in America. Toissin Biongon begged to kindly revive her guardian and her guardian Americans. He asked with tears of Mr. and Mrs. Carter bring to life. But, alas, the two Americans were not as biongonistes Toissin. They were under the protection and benevolence of his worshipers Biongon makes immortal and invincible. They were Christians. They worshiped the God who gives death to sinners. Thus the very long and fervent prayers of Toissin were unsuccessful.

Of Carter's funeral which took place at home, Toissin met several African students. Bernard, Pierre, Jacques Roger, Fabrice Georges, Cornelius and Josiane. Jacques, the Burkinabe, who went to America via the Ivory Coast, Toissin invited to visit her home. He lived in a building in Dorchester, on the second floor, with his black American wife. Toissin responded favorably to this invitation fraternal and friendly. Thus the two men met on a Sunday morning before the camp of Roxbury.

Toissin and arrived at Jacques. The visit had two purposes: to present Toissin Community of Africans in Boston (CAB) and celebrate the arrival of Toissin America. It was the habit or tradition of Africans in America. The African Community of Boston (CAB) and recorded his 413th member of the current year. Its members came from almost all regions of Africa. Northern, central, southern, western and eastern. That Sunday, there were more Africans in Jacques sixty five black American whose wife of Jacques.

Toissin was the Angels in a great world came to welcome the brotherly and devoted African-American. He passed and, symbolically, the American characters with whom he was living in a world completely new to him. We went out so the "bushman" Ivorian its scenery. It is civilizing and Americanized it with music, drink, food, cigarettes, drugs, sex and games. The atmosphere of this place was festive, cheerful, relaxed, cheerful and colorful. Everything was developed for the success of the ceremony. For food, there was at all: Kentucky Fried Chicken, frenchfried, hamburger, cheeseburger, hot dog, scrambled-egg etc.., Etc.., Etc.. Nothing but a wide variety of American specialties. To drink, there were fruit juice, dyes, pasteurized milk, whiskey, rum, beer, wine, champagne etc.. It was enough to honor the philosopher Ivory Coast, to please him and even to dazzle. For, when he saw that since he was born, if it was not in Boston? So much goodness and love! "Ah! America the great and beautiful! America, the beautiful! You are so beautiful! You are amazing! "Exclaimed from time to time Toissin, amazed. He ate everything, drank a little while, smoked a little of everything, danced a lot. He danced on the tunes of Lionel Richie, Barry White, Michael Jackson etc..

About 17 hours, he drank a glass of fruit juice special, very special. A few minutes later, everything was spoiled for him. What? "" The African bushman had a sudden dizziness and a headache very severe and unbearable. For him, the whole building, everyone and all things stir, turned violently and collapsed.

He started in all directions and suddenly the world and faced all the objects in the house. He ends up rolling on the ground spread itself and going in all directions, surrounded by revelers crying like a kid and delusional. He was almost mad. He vomited, urinated on him endlessly and chia. What a shame! This triggered a storm of laughter. "The bushman! The bushman! The bushman! It's funny! He died! He died in America in our hands! Ship it to Abidjan in the first plane from Boston to Africa!"

And people laughed at him. It was really ridiculous and very humbled. He was dragged to the bathroom floor. There he was abandoned and forgotten. He gave everything he had completely eaten and drunk through the mouth and anus. Then he spurred a very deep sleep that kept him in the toilet until the next morning at seven o'clock. When he awoke, he asked Jacques if he was in Abidjan, Ivory Coast, Africa, to Domolon in Gwa countries. "No, my new American poor. You are always and indeed in America and Boston. Now you have become African-American. You are a true A.A. (African American). Now your name is Williams. Ok? Forget some names Toissin, Abidjan, Ivory Coast, Africa, Domolon, etc. Gwa. You need to think now Williams, Boston, Massachusetts, New England, New York, Washington, Chicago, Dallas, etc. ... The sheep graze the grass only where it is attached. You need to be like this: thou shalt be happy. Be chameleon adapts to the manners down quickly from here. In Rome, do as Rome. With wolves, must howl. Otherwise, you will be devoured. Are alike come together. Birds of a feather flock together. This is the best philosophy of happiness, success, salvation for all and everyone. I learn nothing from the philosopher you are. It is a fraternal and friendly simple advice that I give you. We just rename you here. You just revived in America. We've all been this nice event for us culturally integrate into American society. You are obliged to accept it, otherwise you will leave in Africa. That's all. "A philosophical answer this expeditious Jacques to his question, Toissin understood that he was always taken to the test of violence, cultural and axiological fighting (combat values and civilizations). He found himself again facing defense lawyers of American values who asked him to abandon his native culture, all ways of living, thinking and acting in Africa. Philosophical-sociological struggle. Welfare problems, hurt, happiness, success, health, salvation, alienation, freedom, right, duty, cultural relativity and axiological had just posed to him openly and cruelly. Him, philosopher specializing in these issues, found himself challenged.

"What! Baptism, rebirth, Americanization, chameleon, sheep, wolf, Rome, birds, adaptation, etc.., Etc.., Etc..,. What does that mean all that? So I came to your dirty school of philosophy here? What is your speech mean? Do you think I'm here to make me change for America instead of change America really and absolutely deserves to be changed? Do you know who you're talking like this? I am not at all like you. I'm totally different from you guys. I have plans and ambitions noble and glorious for America. You will know soon. I came not to take something to America, but I came to give something bright in America. I am not selfish. Do you understand me? Now, answer my question. Your speech of common man miserable and selfish means what?" Made Toissin, furious at having been humiliated, assaulted and tortured. "It means that you come to live here with me. You celebrated, sleep, vomit, shit. That's all that," said Jacques. Toissin and added: "But how all this happened to me? I want to know everything." Jacques said: "It's very simple to understand. This is your last glass of tini it all happened. "Toissin tended more and more ears to him and asked again: "So what was there in that glass? "Jacques:" There was a nice little tablet. It was he who put you K.O "A piece of veil had been lifted. But there were still many gray areas." A drug? What do we call this sweet little tablet and why did you do that? "Toissin made very indignant. "You do not need to know its name. I will tell you never. Today or tomorrow. It's my secret to myself. We Africans in Boston, you do what we have done to all Africans who come to us here. It is their baptism. I too have suffered the ordeal of initiation. I have suffered this fate fantastic. This is called Wellcome to America (W.T.A.). Tomorrow, you will do the same thing to other Africans. This will be your turn to use W.T.A. against future arrivals in America. This is the law of life. You take vengeance as you like. Everything depends on you and your philosophy. You will be faced with your conscience. But here is what we do. It is a jungle. We are all here big cats, lions, panthers, tigers, wolves, leopards, cheetahs. You must learn to fight and to be like us. A word, hello! "This baptism cynical and terrifying, far from transforming Toissin, make him lose his African identity and make him forget his mission philosopher-physician (philothérapeute) in America, rather it provides the material on which he was to act powerfully, the anti-values that had to fight to help establish a new civilization, human and healthy America.

The lesson of baptism (WTA) was negative, that is to say, negating positive values, but at the same time, it was valuable because it opened the eyes of Toissin the detestable things, it allowed him to live directly and personally experience of the drug or substance abuse that was a big wound to heal and heal. This lesson was valuable lessons about the dangers facing America and, by extension, all humanity.

CHAPTER 9

In the camp where Roxbury Toissin worked, there were many women, girls, ladies or women who are legally married.

One of them was called Mrs. Johnson (Mrs. Johnson). She was very beautiful. She had a very striking chocolate complexion which attracted many eyes on the street and wherever she went. Her natural hair, which were long enough, hiding her face a little thin with a nice aquiline nose in the middle of two big eyes mesmerizing. His teeth were all white and very clean. Mrs. Johnson had an average size, and was slim. She gave his sympathy, his kindness and any softness in Toissin. She was legally tide and mother of a beautiful boy named Michael. She was talking a lot with Toissin in the day, at the time of rest. She was very fond of news from Africa, the continent of his ancestors. Toissin spoiled her on that plane. It filled her with fantastic stories and fables and moralizing he inherited from his culture and oral literature Akan. Rabbit, rat, spider, monkey, elephant, lion, leopard and python were constantly directed or referred to in these stories, in these fables and legends. Mrs. Johnson was very curious, enthusiastic and attentive to these things. Each time, she held out her pretty ears to Toissin, trying to swallow for most people hear, understand and learn more about Africa. Toissin profited for a long smooch, tenderly and passionately. A pure negro and a negress is amourachaient westernized. It was pathetic. Mrs. Johnson saw in Toissin a moving historical memory and a living symbol of his ancestors and concrete captured somewhere, an African, and cruelly transported, hands and feet shackled, in New England by white slave lawless.

One Saturday afternoon, she proudly led Toissin his family home in Cambridge, not far from the great and famous Haward University. They crossed on foot in the Charles River madly in love, tireless, who hurried to return to their bed by taking the historic bridge scary. Once arrived at the private home of Johnson, Toissin was presented lovingly to its U.S. rival as the" wanted" custom" and the" logic of love in America: "Honey, this is my brand new lover. His name Toissin. It comes from Africa. He works in the same camp as me. He is very friendly, nice and beautiful. He is adorable. It fills me with joy and happiness every day. He can speak English. But he speaks mainly French. Its official language is French. He is speaking. I learn a little French with him for free. It makes me a lot of services. So I decided to spend Saturday night with him. Here and outside, at Prudential Center. There, there is a great jazz concert- blues- gospel. Do you have something very nice to say "? she said. "Yes, of course. I must admit that your lover is really beautiful African and kind. Thank you, sir, you are welcome here. You will take my place right away here. Be at ease, without fear or dread. I see your lover's heart beating very, very hard for you. You know, they say: "everything new is good." My wife will make you very happy. You can count on her and on me. Mrs. Johnson loves you truly and deeply. I leave the house to allow you to have fun and do whatever you want. Goodbye! Good weekend to you both!" When they heard this astounding, Mr Johnson, legal spouse, legal, Mrs. Johnson, lit his beautiful limousine 30m of the house and disappeared. Behind him, the love feast began, she was in full swing in the marital bed. Mrs. Johnson asked Toissin in his room, undressed him quickly and threw it into his red bed very cozy and very wide, surrounded by several giant mirrors. At the foot of this enchanting bed, a large color television showed movies of love as very exciting to decorate the feast of love Toissin and Mrs. Johnson and create the apotheosis. "Toissin, darling, you are African. Does your house, in Africa, what we are doing here, right now, is feasible, normal, authorized? "Was the love which tordillait fun and raved, naked, into the arms of her lover virile. "No, no and no. It's unimaginable. It is absolutely unthinkable. It's impossible. Other places, other customs. For Africans, it is despicable and demonic. In Africa, marriage is primarily based on sexual fidelity. A married woman must have sex with her lawful husband. And the married man, too, should have sex with genital his lawful wife. I confess that I sincerely flabbergasted America. I learn new things and too perverse with everyone. In America, it is organized chaos. Men marry men and women marry women. Legally. Ah! Good God! The married woman can lead her lover to her matrimonial home, to present it to her husband. And it allows his wife to have sex with her lover at home, in bed, without any jealousy. What civilization! That's the American paradise. That's the comment I can make this. I do not condemn anyone and I do not condemn anything because it benefit me right now, "says Toissin. "I think you're very smart and beautiful, my darling. I'm a little Americanized, somewhat, a little every day on my way. This is your second baptism U.S. after that your African brothers from Boston in Dorchester made you and you told me. There, it was a baptism negative. Because they failed to kill you by the drug. Here at home, it's the opposite. It is a baptism positive results in sexual pleasure and sublime romanticism. We both love gods Eros and Venus. We are very dedicated their followers. They bless us and give us all their graces. My darling, you must know that we, the American women are emancipated and independent men and our husbands. I have the full right to do whatever I want, even living under the roof of a man and wearing a wedding ring with him. I did not need his permission to act. I am free. Totally free. You recorded in that time, yourself. I do whatever I like and who I want. I did not accountable to my husband about my trips and my gallant love affairs with other people than himself. My life belongs to me and me alone. We American women have fought long and hard for the right to equality with men. This is now part of our culture and our national history. Our ideologists and philosophers, as Angela Davis and many others, we have informed, assisted and saved from the dictatorship of the male. Today, we enjoy freedom with joy. We'll bite your teeth and we are very happy.

But, alas, it is not yet the case for women from Africa, Europe, Asia and Oceania. Women in these regions remains saddled tyranny, unjust authority, domination, oppression and exploitation of the male. They are subject, docile, weak, cowardly, ignorant, savage and unhappy. I pity them very, very strong. Their fate is very pitiful and very sad. We here in America, the male compatriots who married these women totally ignoring their rights: freedom, dignity, peace, equality, justice, happiness, prosperity. They abuse their ignorance and weakness. This is very dishonest on their part. This is very bad. Thus there is a proper American, just, happy and positive and America wrong, unjust, unhappy and negative. We women feminist, revolutionary, and emancipationists independence, we are fighting hard to change, improve and save America if not, to enlighten the minds that are still in the dark ages.

We want a single American. One in which all women will be united, supportive, intelligent, prosperous, happy, free, emancipated, humane and responsible. America has been so far, the chairmen of the male. This is unfair. We'll fix that, and this injustice. It will, now, women presidents. It will delete the report phallocratic which places man above the woman home. Down with machismo! Long live the féminocratie"!"

The wall of racism and Negrophobia fell with the arrival of Mr. BARACK OBAMA, mulatto, at the White House. Pretty revolutionary symbol. It will take the wall of the male chauvinism also falls. That, my dear, my ideas and positions on political, social, gender, humanitarian, moral and philosophical. Do you accept them, you, pure negro, African, scientist, philosopher, humanist?, "She said. This feminist discourse Toissin allowed to speak and to judge the junta U.S. women.

"You ask me if I accept your ideas and political positions, social, gender, humanitarian, moral and philosophical. Yes and no. I accept your ideas and positions. But this is only the name of our love, sentimental weakness, cowardice, hypocrisy, interest, selfishness. Because I did not want to lose your love now, Your love, your affection, your kindness and generosity which are so useful to me. So I support your struggle and your feminist ideology of the emancipation of women. However, referring to scientific objectivity, the reality principle, history and the principle of cultural relativity, I see a lot of cons-truths, illusions, falsehoods and mental poisons in your statements.

We philosophers, humanists and moralists, we study values. Only values. All human values, social, cultural, spiritual, intellectual, etc.. This is to tell you that I have much to say here, in the area where you are coming. I'll give you a nice little lesson here. The do you want? Anyway, you will forgive me if I offend you in my specialist about. It will be unintended on my part," said Toissin, very hesitant and a little worried. This is easily understood. Love requires. Interest requires. Requires caution.

"Okay, go ahead. I need to be corrected and learn something from you. Especially you, my darling, expert on abstract values. I have not done extensive studies in this area. I confess I know nothing about it. You will be my teacher and volunteer staff. Regardless of what you tell me, I will not be angry. I'm listening." Mrs. Johnson and reassured her learned lover who did not want to risk losing his esteem, his benevolence and move on to the enemy. "All right, darling. This is what I want to hear from you. You are humble, modest and curious. I can now give you my lecture free. You have painted a too glowing, too positive, nay pleasant, American women. And you painted a picture too dark and hellish non-American women, African women, European, Asian and Oceanian you do not even know. What you said American women and non-American women is wrong. Completely false. This is a Manichean dualism a delirious and unfounded. This is absolutely unacceptable for a scientifically and philosophically enlightened mind. For example, you assert dogmatically free and that American women are emancipated, free, independent and happy. This is false. Absolutely False. I have traveled in your country far and wide, in every sense. And I have not seen that. I have not found a single concrete sign of real emancipation, freedom, independence and happiness of the real American woman which thou hast vaunted praised, glorified and praised to the skies. I seriously investigated this topic interests me a lot. I'm currently writing a doctoral thesis in sociology on this issue. The findings of my scientific work is true and unequivocal. The American woman is falsely told emancipated, free, independent and happy. This is pure fantasy. It's the pure vanity and falsehood. Emancipation, freedom, independence and happiness are altogether illusory; it is only verbal. It's a beautiful dream, a wish, a theory or hollow words, empty but are mistaken for realities. This borders on delirium, mythomania and schizophrenia group. It is also a collective narcissism and Manichaeism dangerously fueling the popular imagination and the American mentality. It's part of the culture and the American way of life (american way of life). And that's the name of these prejudices and mistaken beliefs that you have become national American women despise, underestimate, insult women, moreover, other continents, more worthy than you. So you allow yourself to deal with these good women of savages, slaves (their husbands) of subject, docile, cowardly, weak, ignorant of, the unfortunate, pitiful and lamentable. It is wicked and unjust. But in truth, these defects that you assign are rather virtues, qualities that are good for any woman on earth. You need to know today. If these women are really like that, they can only be very happy. They are good and very good. You American women, who are their opposites, you do not do better. You are not happy. If there are comparisons to be made here between the American and other women, this is entirely in favor of the latter. It is not in favor of American. It is a scientific truth. This is not my personal opinion. This is what I observe every day in America. Most women here have the outstretched hand daily to men to live or survive. They do not suffice to themselves. In addition, they have a dishonorable life, dirty, indecent, vicious criminal, pathetic, appalling and very unhappy. For example, prostitutes, drug addicts, lesbians, vagabonds, thieves crooks, evil and other offenders, criminal and marginal. These types of women can be found elsewhere. But to a much lesser extent than in America. The political, administrative, economic, social, cultural and spiritual American has failed entirely. It produces mainly women marginal, dangerous waste and destitute. Women without dignity, without proper social situation, without liability, beggars, single, solitary, can they be called happy, free, independent, emancipated? No. Be serious and good faith in our judgments. In Africa, I have known many women really liberated freely and happily that make no pity and who have nothing to envy American women inexemplaires and condemnable. All African work. Whether in cities or as employees in the informal economy or in the villages as planters, cultivators. Most of them are traders and vendors in the markets, shops, streets. In any case, each does something that allows him to live with dignity. Each African woman wins an honorable life by formal or informal work. There are no unfortunate unemployed, poor and miserable as they are found in America. Except, of course, a few bad apples that mimic western women, perverse and depraved: the prostitutes and other women of easy virtue.

Of women infidelity or adultery is a rare thing that is severely punished by the African society. This is not built in a universal rule, in law or in national custom. In Africa, all women are married legally or customarily. Celibacy of women is condemned. This is unacceptable. It's a shame, as does for a woman to smoke cigarettes, drink alcohol, exposing his body to the public, to shoot pornographic films to wear pants, to deceive her husband with a Another man, want to imitate Western ways of speaking, living etc.. African women are very free. They are not slaves to their husbands. Rather, they are genuinely loved and regarded as goddesses by men. They are worshiped, honored, glorified and magnified by men. This is not the case in America, West. African women are strong, courageous, magnanimous and not weak, cowardly. They are civilized and well educated on the core values and positive in their society observe strictly. So they are not ignorant nor savages. Their fate is not pitiful nor terrible. They are at peace in society, at peace with nature and with their husbands. They are balanced, healthy and holy in their minds. They live in harmony and in perfect harmony with men, with their husbands, with society, nature and the universe. So how do these women, so wise can they be unhappy as the American women who are totally distorted, artificial, insane, vicious, arrogant, vain," rebels,"""" anarchists, women who do want not women, wives, mothers etc..?

CHAPTER 10

After his telephone conversation with Mrs. Obama, Toissin felt compelled to work hard to make it actually lives up to its double science (and féminologie philothérapie) he must now teach a very distinguished public and places the most prestigious of the earth. He could not sleep. Day and night and everywhere he worked and read because he was aware he would not have it easy, it would be judged very harshly by the circles, institutes, and American academies. It should provide proof of ad hominem reputation and successfully defend his dual capacity as a scholar and sage. It was highly anticipated on the land by his peers and its U.S. competitors. It provoked too much curiosity in the audience. The framework chosen to host its first major conference was the White House. This place was imposed by the First Lady, Mrs. Obama, became his de facto partner and collaborator.

One month prior to the conference, formal invitations were launched. Communiqués were broadcast regularly every day by all television channels, all newspapers and all radio stations with a brief presentation of Toissin and his work. All this prepared the way for a hit at the conference held on a Saturday afternoon, from 14 h 00. It was in a very large room with sound designed to house very large political meetings and cultural events of great importance. Room well decorated and equipped with machines and instruments of communication and various sophisticated hyper-performance. She drove the world. The very strong advertising, which was made for this conference, gave Americans of all walks of life in the White House. You could see in the dense crowd of scholars, students, teachers, politicians, journalists, photographers, men and women of culture, business, religious and so on. Toissin finally entered the room in a dazzling light and a thunderous applause that expressed general enthusiasm. Here, one might believe in a Michael Jackson concert in public. He was comfortably installed in a golden chair in front of several microphones and silver very well adjusted. At his side were the president and secretary general of the National Association of Women American Feminists (NAAW). On the left, in the VIP, found themselves the First Lady and her illustrious husband surrounded by their numerous bodyguards and some very discreet and military spies. Besides them, all the foreign ambassadors accredited in the country. Toissin saw the ambassador of his country, Ivory Coast, among them, who stared straight in the eye. This gave him both a little flyer and courage to work well. The attentive gaze and its ambassador was his psychological drug, its exciting and challenging.

According to the official protocol in use in such circumstances, Toissin was to be presented, at the outset, the organizers of the event or by the protocol service of the White House. Thus a very great lady coquettish came to the microphones and threw these words: "Your Excellency, President of the Republic, Ladies and gentlemen, the National Association of American Women (NAAW) is pleased to have you here, on this day. She greets you and sincerely thank you for your massive presence at its first extraordinary conference which is something of cultural re-entry. She welcomes your spontaneous mobilization to its cause and your support for its action. She wants everyone out of here, this afternoon, happy to have got a lot of good things in my head that will help him live his life better and happier. It is the purpose of this conference that will start now. We want to meet this challenge with a man who is both clever and wise. This exceptional man will instruct us and guide us on the path to health, success, welfare, happiness and personal salvation. Thanks to two new sciences which are called Féminologie and Philothérapie. If these two words seem odd or foreign, if this surprises you, it's perfect. Is that you learn something new here with a man who is not American and who is called Toissin. Here it is. He will talk to you. Toissin Doctor, you have the floor. "The lady who introduced the speaker and was the Deputy Secretary General of the NAAW (Ms. Brown).

"Before getting into the thick of it, I would first like to acknowledge and thank all the authorities and eminent personalities who are in this room, who were willing to sacrifice some of their time so full and so valuable to come support me, encourage me and honor me. Thank you, Excellency Obama, President of the United States of America. Thank you, Mrs. Obama, Honorary President of the National Association of American Women. I know it is because of you, to your generosity, your personal efforts and your dedication to the Association, this conference was held here at the White House. Thank you to all the distinguished scholars, scientists and teachers. Thank you, ladies and gentlemen of the press. Thank you, ladies and gentlemen of the conference organizers, thank you to you all.

The work I'm going to do here today will be to introduce a new science. The lady who introduced me to you earlier, Madam Deputy Secretary General of the NAAW, spoke instead of two sciences. She is right. In fact, there are two new sciences twins, inseparable from one another. Their names: Féminologie and Philothérapie. Not to be too long, too tired and bored, I'd rather talk to you, today, the only féminologie. I reserve the philothérapie for later and elsewhere. You know I give lectures rotating throughout America. After here, I will be soon at the Monument, the Capitol then, after Empire State Building in New York, the Prudential Center in Boston, Haward, Yale, Cathedral of Learning Pittsburgh at Madison Square Garden in New York, Chicago, Dallas etc..

To begin the work itself, I must first give you a plan to follow, so you can easily understand my speech. So I will start by showing the subject of the following féminologie in his method and, finally, results. The féminologie is to study the woman. For this science, the woman is a human individual who produced both by nature and society. Thus the woman influences and natural features and influences and social and cultural traits. Its natural features and socio-cultural set it apart from man. Its physiology, its anatomy and morphology make it a separate being who takes pregnancy after sex with a man who carries the pregnancy for nine months, and expelling the child from her body. Biology and genetics explain all this in a very precise, detailed experimental and satisfactory. The man also has his own definitional traits. So I can not confuse the man with the woman. When I see a man, I know it's not a man and a woman.

The company has recreated the woman in her own way by giving it specific traits about his way of living, thinking and acting. See issues of clothing, body care, hygiene, education, marriage, work, the rights and duties. The company with the wife of a state of mind, feelings and emotions. She taught him how it should be, to want, to design and conduct themselves in life. And the woman received values and ideas (or ideals) she practices in her daily life. The woman has a moral, psychological, social, physical and metaphysical clean and precise.

The problem with the féminologie and philothérapie is the unfortunate situation of women in life, his sufferings, difficulties, failures and various ailments that prevent him from being serene, happy and saved. The féminologie - philothérapie identified the main causes of the problems of the woman and found effective remedies to these problems. These causes are the same woman. The woman should know and be able to eliminate saved and happy. These are: the lack of" good manners" with others, lack of" know" thinking," the lack of self-knowledge," the lack of" know" to marry, the lack of" know how to manage a home,"" lack of etiquette with her children."

The happiness of woman is subjected to the knowledge and strict adherence to those things which are laws of life. To be successful, women must fill the void that is in it (the" missing") by acquiring the six qualities that are sorely lacking. This requires hard work she has done on herself, on her personality. It must transform, correct and improve his state of mind, to abandon his negative mindset, toxic, in favor of a positive mindset, disciplined, healthy and holy. Here in the West, the woman is engaged in a fierce fight in a duel, a conflict with the man (male) for the affirmation of his ego. It thus has a belligerent mood, hateful, is jealousy, anger, resentment, revenge, envy, etc.. This is very detrimental to his health, success, happiness and salvation. The woman must cease to be as it is now and all is fine and better for her. It must necessarily replace all mental poisons and viruses by love, altruism, compassion, kindness and goodness to man, she makes peace in his mind, it stops consider the male as his enemy, his rival, rival, like the one that prevents it from being happy and saved. The woman should know that man is inseparable from its complement, his alter ego. This is the self-knowledge or wisdom that it should possess.

So feminism as a struggle or violence of women against men is as dangerous as harmful as his opponent, male chauvinism. In sum sexism (feminism and male chauvinism) is prohibited. It is poisonous mental and social. In the male-female relationships, there is neither master nor slave, neither weak nor strong, nor good nor bad, neither angel nor devil, neither dependent nor independent, nor emancipated or not emancipated. There is only necessary complementarity, interdependence (mutual), bilateral cooperation, fundamental unity, harmony, peace, balance. It is pride, vanity, egotism, selfishness, malice, hatred, resentment, grief, intolerance, animosity, competition, greed, jealousy, envy, greed, and greed that lead the warlike spirit, Manichean, narcissistic, destructive conflicts. We need men and woman marry in love to build together their common happiness. Marriage is a contract of love, trust, tolerance, forgiveness, compassion, altruism, happiness and life together. Now all these things are based on the six laws of female life: the" life skills," the" good manners" with others, namely the" thinking,"" namely the marriage ' ', the" good manners" with her children." the ability to manage a home."

The féminologie-philothérapie studying the various reports and fixes (or situations) of women in the world: woman-company reports, reports wife-husband wife relationship-children, reports woman beautiful family. It also examines the causes and signs sociological, biological and psychological suffering and misfortunes of women. This is called the etiology of suffering and misfortune. And biologically, the féminologie-philothérapie finds negative factors such as illness, fatigue and childbirth. In sociological terms, it reveals factors such as boredom, unemployment, poverty, misery, vice, loneliness, celibacy, the anti-natalism. On the psychological level, she discovered as causes: resentment, hatred, jealousy, anger, resentment, vindictiveness, illusion, ignorance, false knowledge, pride, vanity, mind negative, unhealthy, undisciplined. To succeed in life, be healthy, happy and saved, the woman must overcome all these poisons, all these defects which are in his mind and change his mindset toxic. It must seek his deliverance, liberation, emancipation and independence of the psychological side, vis-à-vis itself and not vis-à-vis the male. His disease has a psychological, spiritual and moral. It must purify the mind, to practice its catharsis and make his own internal revolution. His greatest enemy is itself, it is his way of thinking and feeling. It has to fight itself, fight his own shortcomings and win a victory over herself, on her personal flaws, not man, the male. To do this, it can use the man as a precious and indispensable collaborator servant, not fight it. Finally, know that I have created a firm and philothérapie féminologie here in Washington DC, located just steps from the Capitol. You may at any time to meet me there for your own personal health, success, wellness and happiness. I am always at your service.

Excellency the President of the United States of America, Excellencies Ambassadors, Ladies and Gentlemen, today's conference is now over. Thank you for your patience and for your kind attention. Goodbye! ". Amid deafening applause of a mob and enthusiastic, the Chief of Protocol of the Presidency and leaders of NAAW. came Toissin take by the hand, after alternately kissed on the mouth. They led him proudly near the presidential couple satisfied with his performance and dazzled by his eloquence and his rhetoric. In turn, Mr. and Mrs. Obama shook her hand warmly congratulating him and giving him friendly hugs. "My brother, you are a very proud moment for me, for my wife, my children and for all Americans. You are a gift from heaven for all America. Thank you so much and continues to serve America. God bless you!, "Said the U.S. President and give him a big envelope full of banknotes. A reward estimated at one hundred and fifty thousand dollars. Toissin was pleased to see he had won a great success, to conquer the hearts and minds of America and it now included American stars. Under the glare of the cameras of journalists who filmed passionately and she was stripped of words, ambassadors, senators, deputies, ministers and businessmen came to congratulate him in single-leu leaving him that an envelope full of money that a business card. Gifts of all kinds pleuvèrent in his arms followed by invitations generous and helpful.

Toissin was surrounded by men and women of all who wanted his autograph before leaving the room. For two clock hours, Toissin held America spellbound. He turned positively many hearts and minds. He greatly influenced the American destiny.

CHAPTER 11

After the brilliant Toissin conference at the White House, newspapers, televisions and radios Americans threw themselves into an unprecedented battle for advertising, promotion and lobbying the endless féminologie and philothérapie through all America. It saw the photos of the learned and wise African company of Obama, diplomats, ministers, MPs, senators and business people everywhere. Everyone sang the name of Toissin and wore his picture round her neck. Toissin became a hero and a star of the Yankee nation. He was everywhere and in honor of his many law-philothérapie féminologie walked very, very strong. They drove back the world. Toissin gave lectures in all the top universities of USA and Canada. It was also requested by the European and Asian universities. His books were sold and bought like hot cakes everywhere paradise. It was the best bestsellers in America.

Its second major conference was held at Haward University. It was not without reason. Indeed, Toissin called itself CB (Citizen of Boston). Boston was the city that gave him every chance by opening the door to success, prosperity and glory. And he honored this great and beautiful city of his fame and notoriety worldwide. Boston and throughout the State of Massachussett adored him. The CB itself as the second Martin Luther King and the second was intended as liberator and savior of black America. One week prior to this public lecture, all Boston was parried posters and banners bearing the image of Toissin. It read: "The most worthy son of Boston today, Toissin, speaks to America at 15 pm Saturday 00, at Haward." Or "America will be saved from Boston by Martin Luther King bis, the learned and wise CB who will speak to all Americans next Saturday at 15h at Haward. Appointment not to be missed." Or: "America now has a new hero, a new scholarly and wise. This is Toissin the C.B.. He will speak Saturday at Haward, from 15.00. Hasten to-many. Absentees will be wrong. They will regret it. "Millions of people, young, women, men, old, wore T-shirts proudly displaying the photo of Toissin. And everywhere, everyone was talking about him with fervor and joy. We are jubilant and exultant. In churches, temples and mosques, and prayed regularly for daily that God would grant a long life and all his graces to Toissin. The CB occupied totally and royally every heart and every mind in Boston and throughout Massachusetts. There was seen as a prince or a demigod. All advertisements on television, radio, in print and online photos and operated his initials CB. All products sold in America proudly wearing the CB logo and photo of the new national hero.

Two days before the big event took with Haward, Toissin and Jeanne invited everyone to the great new Boston City Hall located near the Charles River. In this circumstance, the CB was draped in a black suit and wore three-piece red tie. He held in his hands a beautiful bouquet of flowers he gave to his wife Jeanne, a former Ms. Johnson. This was all dressed in white with lots of gold jewelry and diamond cuffs, neck, ears, hair, nose, lips, feet, arms, eyes, fingers, chin, etc. … It was the marriage of gratitude to a brave and intelligent woman who knew Toissin lead straight to success and glory. Toissin had no right to neglect or forget such a woman, a true goddess. Mayor hurried into the room, smiling, with a delay of fifteen minutes. He apologized quickly. The Bostonians were waiting for. In his view, everyone stood up spontaneously and joyfully together, made a quick movement, prompt, courteous, to greet him. A very soft musical tune embellished the solemn atmosphere of the room and relaxed. "Please sit down," said the Mayor. Everyone obeyed. The room became very quiet, peaceful, quiet. The couple Toissin-Jeanne was sitting in the front row right in front of the chief magistrate of the city. In a charming setting that attracted the attention of all, the Mayor delivered the traditional official speech to unite legally Toissin and Jeanne. The "yes" of the two lovers shook strongly support and provoked a storm of laughter and applause in the room. It was very beautiful and pathetic. Jeanne wept for joy and happiness by embracing Toissin and by putting his golden ring on his finger. As for Toissin, he began his height and remained dignified and serene by performing the same gestures.

City Hall, everyone cheerfully and promptly transported in the large party room of the tower Prudential Center. Here, hostesses like cheerleaders, wearing the colors of the new favorite couple (yellow, red, green) in short skirts with blouses, hats, shoes, high heels, stockings, servèrent to eat and drink to the public. They were so lovely, they gave appetite swings to even those who were not hungry. All were in love VIPs and secretly wanted to get married later also. They relied on God for this project pretentious. And some very pleasant and interesting they were politely whispered in his ear. The lucky and daring of them even received invitations, business cards impressive. On each occasion of his friend.

There were all sorts of treats, from appetizers, cake: hamburger, cheeseburger, hot dog, frenchfried, Kentucky fried chicken, fruit juice, whiskey, champagne, sparkling wine, red wine, beer, rum, milk, syrup, etc. … Around 19 hours, the world retreated and grooms could return to their hotel room reserved for gold and specially arranged for their wedding night, for their honeymoon.

This marriage, which took place before the conference Haward, Toissin endowed with a moral force, psychological and legal CB needed to perform properly and legitimately all its glorious mission in America. Now he had a free hand to act fully as any good American citizen who was concerned about the interests of his country. The action of Toissin then enrolled in a patriotic and nationalistic. The marriage gave the blow to U.S. citizenship Toissin. And be an American citizen through marriage, gave freedom of expression, to think and act politically to any alien who was a naturalized American.

The conference Haward, announced with great fanfare, brings together people from all walks of life. Academics, students, scholars, researchers, religious, politicians, journalists and businessmen took part. The Cambridge neighborhood was swarming with people. It was invaded by people he had never seen before and wanted to satisfy their curiosity and learn. The biggest and most beautiful amphitheater Haward vomited world. He declared himself unable to contain a million souls very distinguished and disciplined feverishly waving little white flags in the air to salute and honor a new national scholar. At Cambridge, one heard a single word in every mouth. It was C.B. became a national symbol.

Kenedy in the amphitheater, the mayor of Boston, which sponsored the event, took place alongside the president of Haward. These two figures framed affectionately and solemnly speaker. At 15 o'clock, the President spoke on behalf of the entire University Haward to acknowledge and thank the crowd for his encouraging presence and proven value it gave to the world of culture, thought and Knowledge. He particularly thanked the godfather of his moral, material and financial support to organize this conference. He ended his remarks with a terse presentation of Toissin he regarded as someone who was not present to the American public and, still less, to the people of Boston, "Citizen of Boston, Martin Luther King a, New savior of black America, all this is you, Toissin, the man whose clothing has four colors symbolizing philosophically and morally the four human races (black, white, yellow and red), unity and reconciliation of humanity torn by conflicts of interest. Toissin, humanist, you have the floor. Haward, Boston and all America will listen to you here. "It was enough to trigger a burst of applause in the room hysterical. The packed crowd was impatient and firmly attached to the lips of Toissin won by the leaflet. But, as qu'habitué the crowds, he managed to quickly overcome this little discomfort. "First and foremost, I would first like to acknowledge and thank the organizers of this conference who do me the honor, friendship and pleasure in inviting me here this afternoon to discuss the philothérapie. I salute and thank especially the Mayor of Boston, just recently my marriage officer, and very generous sponsor of this conference very dedicated, and the President and Council of eminent professors, researchers and scholars of the prestigious University of Haward. Ladies and gentlemen, good evening and thank you for coming here to listen to me very many. The theme I will address here is the" philothérapie: instrument for health, happiness and salvation of mankind." Such a theme is very evocative and very catchy. It awoke great interest in everyone. It is very motivational and unleashes a lot of positive passion. It seems natural since these are the values and the most precious and dearest to humanity. Firstly, I must know the nature of the philothérapie. What is it? This is both a science or a complex knowledge and technical expertise as special, life skills and etiquette.

As a science, it provides suitable knowledge that enables the man to know himself perfectly (know-thyself), to understand the world and things perfectly. Thus it effectively fight against ignorance, obscurantism, illusion and error that bully, subjugate and destroy the man during his existence in the world. It aims to change the negative mindset of the common man, to enlighten and guide the steps of the latter by correcting his judgment or his glance Assessor on things and situations that are harmful.

As a special technique or procedure, the philothérapie used to prepare men for their perfect success, to perfect their welfare, their bliss, their perfect health and perfect their salvation. Thus it provides a set of rules, principles and laws constituting the practical wisdom expected by men or the art of mastering life, the human mind and all situations. Science and technology, grouped here under the name of philothérapie, show men who are in search of truth perfect, well perfect, perfect virtue, perfect happiness and perfect salvation, how to think, act and live. We find the philothérapie in Buddhism, Hinduism, Christianity, Taoism, Confucianism, Shintoism, Islam, Epicureanism, Stoicism, "the Afrocratisme," the "féminologie" etc..

What are the objectives of philothérapie? Its objectives are twofold. There is the theoretical goal and objective practice. First, the theoretical target. Here, the philothérapie aims to educate men about the true nature and value of human life, the universe, something concrete and abstract. Thus it is humanism, naturalism, vitalism, cosmology, axiology, eschatology, etiology, metaphysics, theosophy, ethics, psychology, parapsychology, ecology. The philothérapie deals with the relationship between man, the world (the physical environment, natural materials), society, the spirit and values of all kinds. It relies on the know made and supplied by the world for thousands of years (as a science, philosophy, wisdom) that guides and enlightens humanity throughout the earth.

The philothérapie recognizes and exploits the teachings and doctrines from all schools and all world civilizations (Western schools, African and Asian). It promotes open mind about the world and encourages healthy human erudition. Thus, she struggles against ignorance, obscurantism, prejudices, illusions, sectarianism, dogmatism, intellectual or cultural bigotry that are the greatest dangers as a source of all evil in the world. In sum philothérapie teaches the truth or perfect knowledge that serve as guarantees or solid foundation for the daily struggle of men for their success, prosperity, welfare, their happiness and salvation. The instruction given by the philothérapie is practical or utilitarian as it is directed to research the conditions of a better life and salutary.

Its practical purpose. Here, the activity is intended philothérapie ethical, moral and eudémonique. Because it provides a means for man to realize his wishes and achieve its purposes. Indeed, the philothérapie promotes good health, success, wellbeing, happiness and salvation of men. It is an instrument serving the interests of good causes and human. In simple, clear and precise, the technique is philothérapie health (medical art or a method to treat and heal the sick), successful, well-being, happiness and salvation. This practical, or utilitarian, is closely and dialectically linked to the theoretical or intellectual who enlightens, informs, educates people about themselves, about things and the world in general. These two aspects of philothérapie are complementary and inseparable. Indeed, science maintains and nourishes the art or practice by his teachings and laws and, in turn, confirms the validity of the technique, the accuracy, power and merit of scientific knowledge. Medical practice. What is she here? Medical treatment philothérapique proceeds in much the same way that medical treatment of psychoanalytical. To heal their patients, or subjects of repression, that is to say people who suffer from mental disorders, psychoanalysts (Freud) investigate their lives through an interview or conversation. This allows to show the clear consciousness (the ego) of patients the cause of their mental condition, that is to say the element repressed in their subconscious mind (the id) that disrupts. The healing principle here is simple: to tell the patient the event of his life (forgotten, ignored or not) which makes him sick. And once it becomes aware of this event (the cause of his illness, because hidden within himself, in his mind), he receives advice from his attending physician, who led him to leave his state toxic mind, to adopt another way of thinking, behaving, of living life psychological or mental. The patient's physician obtains a change of mental attitude, that is to say, he passed it to his negative mindset, toxic, a positive mindset, healthy and wholesome. This is the secret (or method) healing successfully applied by clinical psychologists and psychoanalysts.

The philothérapie shows how to bring men to think, act and live positively to be happy, and saved to succeed and prosper in life. It reveals the rules, principles or laws of the world, of life, the human mind and all situations to know and respect to control life, spirit, and the situations surrounding world. The great principle of philothérapie is to get people to discipline his own mind perfectly, and to be everywhere at all times positive, that is to say, to have his mind healthy and holy. For proper operation, good management and good use of his mind (or art have the ability to think positively) derived the well-being, success, happiness, good health and salvation of all.

In our first manual philothérapie include 41 laws or rules to be applied to life, the world, to oneself, to different situations and its spirit. These are recipes and practical methods needed. Its title: the golden rules of success, health, happiness and personal salvation.

To conclude this conference, let me recall the essential things that I say. The philothérapie is a new art that serves to heal and save the sick, to help people succeed in life and be happy with the philosophy. Here the philosophy is understood as a collection of tips and lessons drawn from different doctrines and different areas. These lessons have the particularity to reveal the laws of life, of the human spirit and rules to guide people to success, good health, happiness and salvation. A philothérapeute is someone who cares for and heals the sick by transforming their negative thinking (toxic and poisonous) or poor state of mind by philosophical advice. How does he define philothérapeute disease and illness and how he treats his patients? What are the means by which he? For philothérapeute, the disease is a poor physical and mental health to be resulting in the suffering, pain, imbalance and physiological disturbances, mental and social. For him, a patient is an individual who is in a bad mood or is someone whose body, life and thought are poisonous and which, therefore, suffers in his mind, in its body and in her life. Is anyone whose quality of mind and life is bad. For philothérapeute, most humans are sick. The disease is a universal state which has two main forms. One form is as false that we carry in our minds. This false knowledge consists of ignorance, falsehood, delusion, error. It is our false or wrong way to think of all things, beings, the world and ourselves. For example, our vision of ourselves and loved, which insulates and contrasts things and makes them believe that things are independent of each other and they have an intrinsic existence, absolute or autonomous (or that every is in and of itself) is false and illusory. The truth is exactly the opposite of this design. Indeed, all beings are interdependent and mutually interacting and form a unity existing in a single large Everything in the universe.

The other form of disease consists in the presence of mind destructive feelings and emotions as anger, hatred, jealousy, envy, fear, pride, remorse, shame, anxiety etc.. These things are our worst enemies at home because they poison our lives and our relationships with others and make us very unhappy. They often are born of dissatisfaction and discontent that are also highly toxic. So anyone know who gives false or harmful is feeling sick. She is mentally disturbed and intoxicated. The lack of serenity, balance and harmony" within itself. His healing and well-being, happiness and salvation lie in its issue vis-à-vis the false knowledge and disturbing emotions and culture, for it, compassion, kindness, love and of liberating meditation. "Mens sana in corpore sano and sancta," one might say in Latin (a healthy mind and holy in a healthy body). Ladies and gentlemen, is this word that ends the conference date. Thank you for your kind attention."

CHAPTER 12

One month after the unforgettable conference Haward, America was attacked. She was attacked at different places by U.S. airliners. They were led by terrorists Alqaïda. The big and beautiful and all-powerful America Métissé new President (born of a father and a Native American- Chinese mother, whose name was Chinindien) was outstanding. She lived the ordeal, the Apocalypse and Hell. The Americans were inconsolable. They were terrified, confused, anxious, angry, hateful, panicked. President Chinindien had temporarily fled the country. He took refuge in Canada for fear of being bombed and killed. There were several thousand deaths in one day in Washington DC, Pittsburgh and New York. The twin towers known as The World Trade Center in New York collapsed one after another, after being violently collide with two planes that followed. America was in mourning.

When President Chinindien reappeared later on television, he cried out vengeance. He was enraged. He promised to retaliate, to hunt down and kill the perpetrators, accomplices and instigators of the Apocalypse. Around the world. He promised to avenge America and respond with the war against Afghanistan, Iraq, Pakistan and the entire Arab and Muslim world where the fighters could hide Alqaïda. The head of the patron of the Arab terrorist organization, bin Laden, was a price. The latter was wanted in the world by the CIA with all employees and employees of all races, all religions, all nationalities and all conditions. War was raging. The Constables of the earth or Cowboys were present in all the countries on all continents. They successively invaded Afghanistan, neutralizing the Taliban leadership,

Iraq by hanging its President Saddam Hussein, Pakistan where, using unmanned aircraft, UAVs, they bombed and massacred night and day, and any time, men, women, innocent children and the elderly in the cities and villages.

The Yankees called these wars, preemptive wars, wars of democratization, liberation and civilization. In fact, wars were illegitimate, arbitrary, imperialist, capitalist for colonization, cultural domination and exploitation of the wealth of the Arab world. And found the trick to this was the false pretext and wacky that it had rid the world of International Terrorism (creation of the Yankees), impose liberal democracy, development (what development?), Respect for Human Rights, man (any man Which human?), modernity or Western civilization and happiness (how happy?) to the world, all the earth. It was in this climate of violence, injustice, arbitrariness and extremely tense political and psychological Toissin was officially invited by the U.S. federal government, under the personal initiative of President Chinindien, to give a lecture the Capitol. " The right man in the right spot and in the right time" (the right man in the right place and right time). Toissin felt himself honored to the last degree. The large and beautiful American, who was suffering, in trouble, in crisis and war against the universe, nature, earth and mankind its lessons waiting to be saved and happy. What glory for a negro and an American citizen abroad through marriage!

The CB was apparently satisfied and proud of himself. Indeed, just simple and ordinary man in his place would have fired legitimately pride, pleasure and joy of it. Toissin but was not a man to do that. Toissin was not an ordinary or vulgar to indulge in such a harmful practice. It was he, specifically, who advised all men not to feel emotions and destructive feelings such as pride and vanity. Thus, there still remained calm and unruffled. He deserved so much for the invitation" a" one-man show at the Capitol. At any Honour to whom honor.

The new President in war really needed wisdom and philothérapie. Him whose wife was a product of the intersection of all races in the world (breeds black, yellow, white and red). Extraordinary product. Toissin described the First Lady as a mysterious with yellow head, red face, the four black and white trunk. It represented so many enigmas and symbols to decipher, to decode and decipher. The synthesis of the world? Beings? Humans? Values? It was a big secret natural, cosmic and divine. Why has there four races? Why not more? Why not less? Why has he humanity? Rather than nothing? What is the purpose of humanity? If humanity does not exist, as would happen in the world? Philosophers, theologians and scholars have provided different answers to these and many questions. Toissin was based on their teachings to educate and save the Americans. He used much of the science of metaphysics and theology. Indeed, the philothérapie is an association or synthesis of several disciplines. Thus Toissin was a versatile man, a kind of omniscient really interesting. He had perfect intellectual, moral and spiritual wisdom that were beneficial for the Greeks, Hindus, Chinese, Africans and other peoples of antiquity. Toissin was a contemporary of those who inherited it. And he wanted to put this precious heritage at the service of the Capitol. The day fixed for the conference was a Thursday. Is it by chance effect? No. Chance does not exist. Everything is determined. Everything is explained. Thursday was for the ancient Romans, a day dedicated to the worship of their greatest god, Jupiter. This one was perched on a hill called the Capitol. Thursday means literally the day of Jupiter (Jovis dies in Latin). The U.S. Capitol, which housed the conference, was built after the Roman model.

For the Romans, the Capitol was a temple. For the Yankees, it's a political edifice (National Assembly). Does religion have anything to do with politics? Yes. Religion and politics necessarily meet. They influence each other. Indeed, the command is an activity of God. This is a purely and exclusively divine. This means that men must govern themselves according to the rules and moral and spiritual laws that God has dictated. The power comes from God. It is sacred. Only God really governs the whole world he created. But sometimes it delegates some of its infinite power to certain people (the elect) so that they represent the earth and help in his task. He asks them to do His will among men in society, nature and the universe. This is the mission of kings, emperors, leaders, presidents, prime ministers, MPs, senators, ministers, mayors… This is the meaning of politics. This is the rationale for the policy.

A secular political, atheist, materialist, is absurd, foolish, absurd and totally unreasonable. It leads to all kinds of disasters, wars, crises in all directions, all misfortunes (poverty, poverty, disease, unemployment, suffering, devastation, disaster, etc..). This is the sad fate, the fate of the macabre political modernity, politics secular, materialist and atheist.

All governments should act solely in the name of God (Deus, Theos, Brahman, Atman, Krishna, NIAMIEN, Yékin, Lago, Gnonsoa, Allah, Mazda). They are accountable to God. They have bills to make it. A king and a president are sacred mission to lead their people to Paradise Divine, the greatest happiness and salvation. All true national policy is theocracy in its pure sense, original and authentic. Combat theocracy by modernity and secularism, and it's slipping off the rails. Policy secular and materialistic whites is artificial, illegitimate, ineffective and dangerous because it is outside the single source of wisdom that is God (light). Thus it is violent, unjust, arbitrary and immoral. It operates on the basis of the crime, the crime and sin.

Laws passed by parliament on Capitol Hill are inspired directly by God, Jupiter (Zeus in Greek), very jealous of his temple. So Americans have officially proclaimed on their national currency, they believe in God (in God we trust). It is very good (very good). They are right. Arab theocracies (Iran) are also right. African monarchies also have non-secular reason. In any case, man can not turn our backs on God and be happy and safe. Man is condemned to follow the teachings and laws of God are the way of wisdom and therefore, the way of salvation. Secularism and atheism are fatal errors.

Thursday, July 4. Holiday for all America. The anniversary of American independence. Day chosen for the conference at the Capitol. It therefore entered directly in the official program of festive events grandiose. This gave the blow to the Toissin official status of an official who was speaking to parliamentarians and to all American leaders. This was intended to settle down and reconcile them with the god Jupiter (they did not always) in his temple very, very, very sacred and very, very, very holy. It was an opportunity for Toissin psychoanalyze the Yankees and turn them into saints, purify and sanctify their minds and heal their collective disease, multiple and diverse: hatred, animosity, anger, contempt, superiority complex, of size, developed for industrial, power, world policeman, civilized, wealth, revenge, bitterness, resentment, etc.. etc.. etc.. Too many to cure diseases. Too many mental poisons or viruses to destroy the CB to fill save Americans at war everywhere in China, Korea, Vietnam, Afghanistan, Iraq, Pakistan, Iran, Libya, Liberia, Cuba, Latin America, Africa, on Venus, Mars, the moon, in the Sahara desert etc.. Imperialist wars, colonial, globalizing, preventive, démocratisatrices, libéralisatrices, civilizing, ANTI-TERRORISM, etc. developmentalists. Too many wars at once, then it takes even one, then it should be practiced only the absolute non-violence (ahimsa in Sanskrit) taught by Asian Buddhists, Yogis, Hindoos, Taoist and Confucian, which does so much good. His Holiness the Dalai Lama (Tenzin Gyatso M.) does it not doing its job of spiritual and moral education in America? He who preaches day and night for decades and moral philosophy of nonviolence in order to lead the Yankees to nirvana, the state of Buddhahood, the state of spiritual awakening, the Moksha. The devil Samsara (the opposite of moksha) and collective negative karma (the law punitive, corrective cause and effect) they retain the Yankees-Cowboys forever prisoners of misfortunes?

It was 16h GMT. The Capitol was stormed. It was packed. All Ministers, Senators, Governors, Deputies, Ambassadors from around the world and all the staff of the White House had gathered at the Capitol to listen to the CB The Mayor of Washington DC, Mr. Darkness took the first speech to acknowledge and thank the distinguished guests, and provide assistance remarkable Toissin. He was followed by the Minister of Culture, Mr. Warrior situation that assistance on the timeliness and relevance of the event. He ended his speech by giving voice to the CB, very concentrated and attentive to everything that is said and done in the room. President Chinindien Toissin stared into his eyes. He was trying to impress her, to seduce him and convince him by the magnetism that drew its pretty robe embroidered with four colors (red, white, black, yellow). It was an enigma, a symbol difficult to decipher, to decode and decrypt by the audience. He walked majestically to the microphone, with lots of charisma and began: "Your Excellency, the President of the United States of America, very honorable Members, Senators, members of the Government, Your Excellencies the Ambassadors, ladies and gentlemen, I fraternally and cordially greet all in the name of Peace and Love. You and I are all working together here for our peace, serenity, our health, our success, our happiness and salvation perfect. Yes, that's what we do. This is what it is here. The philothérapie deals only with that. She did it the subject of study and experience. We are in a holiday. America celebrates its traditional July 4th, historical and sacred date of its accession to independence. This national independence was hard-won through violence legitimate, justified by the war. Today is a glorious, poetic and beautiful. We celebrate a beautiful and great military and political victory over England, colonizer and founder of America. Originally from that country, was war. The war against the Red Indians. The war helped build this beautiful, big, powerful and rich countries. The war also helped to free America from British rule. But that does not mean we can not do without war. Indeed, the war is not inevitable. It is determined by causes controllable by situations, psychological laws and specific socio-historical. If these conditions of possibility and achievement disappear, if they no longer exist, once the war depends on it, also disappears. It is very important and very useful for the war, even justifiable and defensible never exists. Instead of war, it is always best to restore peace. It is in the interest of everyone to cultivate peace, not only war ever. For the violence of war is too harmful. It's too bad. It only evil. What she seems to like happiness is in fact an illusion of happiness, an illusion of happiness. One can obtain genuine national independence without ever making war. President Felix Houphouet-Boigny took independence for the Ivory Coast, his country, without making war on France, colonizing country. This is one example among many others in Africa and other continents. We must do everything to avoid war. No war of colonization, no war no war decolonization and independence. The war is harmful in every respect. It has no real benefit in the background. It destroyed physically, materially, intellectually, morally, spiritually and psychologically. It leaves indelible scars on the country harmful making it and its inhabitants.

America has seen too many wars. The war of colonization, the Revolutionary War, the Vietnam War, World War, the war against the

Muslim Arab countries etc.., Etc.., Etc. ... It is too! To stop. We must now build the health, success, welfare, peace, harmony, happiness and salvation of Americans. Currently, the American collective karma is very negative. The U.S. will be very dark. But we must do so that it shines. And very strong. I personally use this. This is my small contribution. I finally determined the critical issue of sexism. At least, I believe. I also set the burning issue of racism. Through my teaching every day and through many conferences I have spoken, the virus is dead racist. I killed him. America has a President today both India and China. This is Chinindien. His predecessor, Mr. OBAMA, I see in this room all smiles, is both black and white. It's so beautiful! This shows that there is more racism or racial discrimination in American politics. It's so beautiful and I am very, very proud.

The current U.S. problems or diseases of national and collective here, we must fight now, are imperialism and capitalism. These two evils are expressed by illegitimate and immoral the desire of domination and exploitation around the world. This is inspired by pride, contempt, hatred, vanity, greed, greed, malice, passion, and the complex of grandeur, wealth, power, etc. development. All this has led America into an impasse, the disarray and confusion. So we talk about infinite crisis, unlimited political crisis, financial crisis, economic crisis, social, cultural crisis, crisis mental, psychological, spiritual etc.. At the end when all of these crises? When will happiness for all? When is the salvation for all? When will the good health for all? When is success for all? None of this can be achieved only if transform the American way, to change the negative mindset of Americans today, to eliminate all viruses mental or psychological poisons that are ravaging. America must abandon its policy negative current highly toxic. In this case the evil, barbaric violence and its ignoble against other states and other innocent people who want to live in peace, happy, free, prosperous without being slaughtered, murdered, exploited, dominated, or plundered by person home. America must remain only in America must deal with personal problems, internal and respect the right of others to live, act and think according to their own values, their own styles, their own cultures and their own traditions philosophical, religious, political, economic and social.

America must learn to respect the dignity of all beings, animate and inanimate, visible and invisible to every person and every people.

She must know that the life of every individual, human, animal, vegetable, mineral or each element of nature, the universe, the cosmos is sacred, as a work of God, Allah, Brahman, Ishvara, Atman, Yékin, Lago, NIAMIEN… (multiple and diverse names of God in the World Languages). America should stop making war everywhere, kill, kill and kill unfairly, arbitrarily, those it considers to be wrong (ignorance or bad faith) as sworn enemies, and enemies to life deadly enemies: the Taliban, terrorists international Islamist fundamentalists, Muslims, communists, socialists, Marxists-Leninists, Maoists, Stalinists… America must know that all beings in the world are brothers. America must know that all beings are interdependent, fundamentally united by a single destiny. America must know that all beings share the same goal: happiness. This happiness can be achieved by each individual or each people by their behaviors, feelings and thoughts positive. Happiness is to humans and all States fully respect the rights of others, that is to say the cardinal values, universal, inalienable freedom, peace, security, justice, equality, fraternity, friendliness, love, compassion, altruism. America needs to live fully and completely its motto or slogan contained pompously and ostentatiously on its national currency "In God we trust" (in God, we believe). It is very good (very good). Yes, we must believe in God. Sincerely. VERY SINCERELY. Respecting its commandments and sacred laws that impose the values already mentioned. Ladies and gentlemen, it is useless for me to speak here too. I have said enough. What I have said enough to correct and improve the fate of America if it is heard, understood, appreciated and applied. I actually said essentially that I needed to say in this place before so prestigious and so many VIPs in front of so many individuals from the highest social rank, and before his Excellency the President of the United States of America. All that honors me greatly. It honors me very, very strong. To the point that I wonder if I could fully meet the expectations of all Americans here. Do I have accomplished the mission that my country, America, has entrusted to me for this day solemn and memorable? Thus ended the conference here and now. Thank you for your kind attention. "Thus ended the lecture of philothérapie for the Federal government. During this long awaited went in the ears, nostrils, eyes, mouths, stomachs, hearts, lungs, minds and hair of the Yankees. Toissin was proud to have played its role as the new U.S. citizen zealous, patriotic, loyal and nationalistic. Instead of a thunder of applause which America simple, ordinary was so used in such circumstances, rather Toissin was greeted by silence paradoxically disapproval.

It was present at the Capitol in an Apocalyptic conference icy, heavy and disturbing. No evidence of joy, pleasure and satisfaction was evident on a face in the room. We saw rather expressions of anger, indignation and discontent on their faces. The room was buzzing and growling. Rumblings were becoming increasingly vocal in the back of the room. It quickly won the middle and then the whole room. Toissin, who thought he had worked hard and done his duty to America, was soon persuaded otherwise. He realized he had seriously offend America. He realized that he had mortally wounded by an American official discourse too outspoken, too direct, too true, frankly, straightforwardly, without diplomatic cowardice or hypocrisy. Toissin and was the sad experience of the adage: all truths are not good to say (or truth is not good to say). But how the wise and caring he was he could not tell all the truths that were needed to solve American problems? Since his speech was to give peace, good health, welfare, safety, happiness and salvation to the Americans. His speech (his truth) is the appropriate remedy (panacea) to American evil. When one wants to cure a patient, should be absolutely fine diagnose his illness, to disclose all the root causes and the specific nature of the pathogens that attack and then to propose an adequate and effective therapy, that is ie the remedy that is capable of removing the causes of evil and to give healing. Any sick body must be treated by a brave, brave to (honest means Toissin language Gwa Ivory Coast), an intrepid, that hurts, operates the diseased organ necessarily suffer by the patient and useful. That's medical practice. She has no mercy for the sick because she loves them, wants their property, their health, happiness and salvation. She is forced to be mean or cruel to be able to save patients and be more useful. His cruelty at it's humanism. The caregiver (the philothérapeute) and is a humanitarian, a good man, a sage, a servant of God and the world. It does its job without kindness, without light, without cowardice, without hypocrisy, without fear or weakness. He has a special moral, ethical and legal code specific. It has its own logic and philosophy to which the rule of efficiency. He is pragmatic. For him, the end justifies the means and all truth is good to be said that it will cure a disease and save lives. This is the way of gold or the royal road. Is senseless, anyone who thinks otherwise.

But in the Capitol, the politics was triumphant. She tried to wring the neck of healthy science and philosophy. Politicking sulked science and tried to choke, strangle or cause him to lie for his unhealthy pleasure. The politician is dishonest demagogue. This is a deceiver and a cheat. It seeks a science that flatters and caresses him in the direction of hair growth. He likes to use everyone and everything for his diabolical, demonic and satanic. Thus, it wants a science that celebrates and makes propaganda for his eternal hold on power. Its main objective is the stability of his regime. And now the philothérapie thwarted this obscure design. Thus philothérapie became the enemy of American politicians who could not bear her sharp truths and sprayers. The Capitol was soon emptied into a tumult of indignation and protest indescribable. A lady who was next to Toissin spat in his face before leaving. A gentleman who followed the lady slapped the CB on the mouth. Another man gave him a violent kick to the chest. Another sent him a nasty punch to the face. Toissin then collapsed on the ground vomiting blood. His two eyes were gouged out. His tongue was cut off and thrown out, his ears were torn, her sex was removed and taken away. His ten toes were crushed. He was rushed to the nearest hospital in a comatose state. Later, having regained consciousness, he remembered the words of the President of the United States of America, had to leave the room hurriedly before the end of the conference: "Bye! Bye! Take care of your self! " (Goodbye, take care of yourself!) Usual formula is said to everybody when we left. But on Capitol Hill, Toissin gave him another meaning in mind what happened to him: "Goodbye, my poor scholar-care! Be careful what you say because if you continue like that, get into trouble. At your peril."

The C.B. may have reason. For the First State Hospital (the first public hospital) where he was received, the U.S. President said: "My dear scholar-caregiver, you have missed completely in tact, caution and political wisdom. In this environment, there is a decent behavior to hold. We do not say things in a raw, direct and loud. Must comply with the protocol in use. It is important not to hurt the sensitivity and susceptibility of people. You must speak with caution, restraint and kindness. Everything must be measured, monitored all his words, be polite, courteous, friendly and diplomatic. It must flatter the people, instead of blaming them, vilify them, denounce them and condemn them. One must consider the self-esteem, dignity, pride, vanity and pride of the people. For us, policy, conduct or the proper education of a citizen is above science, medicine and philothérapie. I have personally found that you ignore all that and you want to put your knowledge and your medical art above us and America as a whole. This is a fatal mistake. It does not work like that. And these are the consequences. I sincerely regret what happened to you. I sympathize with your pain. But it's your fault. It is you who provoked. That said, I wish you a very speedy recovery. May God help thee and save thee from death. I pay all costs of your hospitalization. In this regard, I have already given instructions as appropriate and adequate means to those responsible for this hospital. On your way out of here, come see me directly to the White House. I personally support your struggle humanitarian. My prédecessaire, President BARACK OBAMA and his wife, gave you all your chances. Me, I must reinforce that to make you happier. Goodbye!."

CHAPTER 13

In the aftermath of the tragic events at the Capitol, newspapers, television and radio stations entered the controversial American politician, moral and scientific. The press had its lambsquarters. Some journalists chose to judge Toissin politically. Others preferred to judge morally. Still others chose to try him scientifically. In the headlines, one could read this:

"Toissin, the wise false, false healer and sorcerer African was killed yesterday on Capitol Hill."

"The CB has paid with his life for his recklessness and arrogance." "Toissin the philothérapeute that claims to save mankind was shunned, spat upon and physically assaulted yesterday at the Capitol:

his condition is very critical."

"The scientific truths and moral lessons of Toissin disturb the government and the American State: tragedy and scandal on Capitol Hill yesterday."

"Very dirty time for CB: greatness, fame and misery and deprivation." "Toissin came out of Paradise to enter Hell."

"Toissin: the glory of the supreme humiliation." "The Capitol sulks, and disavows Toissin runs." "Toissin is at a crossroads."

"C.B. on his cross. He became Jesus."

"Toissin proved yesterday on Capitol Hill, he is a friend of the robbers, terrorists and an associate of bin Laden."

"Toissin says he is a communist, socialist, Marxist-Leninist and Stalinist."

"The CB is anti-capitalist, anti-liberalism and Islamism."

"Toissin is a dangerous man for America: it asks Americans to love their worst enemies terrorists, Islamists, communists, socialists, Marxists-Leninists like themselves. Poor!"

"Toissi out! You deserve death or life imprisonment."

Each gave its interpretation and commentary of the event. Toissin was not as enemies. He also had friends. There were also people neutral towards him: neither friends nor enemies. People in scientific and objective judgment. It was high quality and validity of his impeccable and undeniable science and practice féminologique philothérapique that interested them. It only mattered to them. After finding so much denigration, defamation and malice towards him, Toissin decided to defend themselves through a press conference. He wanted to turn the tide and return the situation to his advantage. It was the most perfect opportunity for his many enemies and detractors to come to overwhelm her leading questions and accusatory.

The place chosen was Empire State Building, a skyscraper in New York very impressive. One Friday in the afternoon. All the country's journalists were present. The room was full. The idea of this conference aroused much curiosity. People wondered what was going Toissin say about the event from the Capitol, on his new life, on his knowledge and practice féminologique philothérapique, etc. on U.S. policy., Etc.., Etc.. At 16:00, Toissin stood boldly before his guests excited and the press conference began: "Ladies and gentlemen of the press, good evening! I sincerely thank you for answering these and many of my call here, on this day, to exchange ideas with me on my situation and on the American news about me. You all know who I am and what happened to me Thursday, July 4 at the Capitol, the anniversary of American independence. I gave a lecture that day as an official guest of the American state. I had to freely express my opinions on U.S. problems with solutions philothérapiques because that is why I was invited to this place. Then, you know. One has afflicted me with physical abuse, physical punishment may take my life. My physical is very serious injury. Currently, I am physically disabled. I lost my eyes, my ears, my nose, my sex, my tongue, my fingers and my toes. But thanks to the philothérapie, I am still alive and I was able to establish a new body that allows me to live somehow and acting. This new body is invisible to ordinary men, for the uninitiated like you the great mysteries and mystical secrets taught by philothérapie. So I see, I hear, I smell, I have a language, I have ten fingers, ten toes, penis, more efficient, more powerful and more sensitive than my old natural physical bodies.

I have read and listened to your comments and tendentious interpretations of my unhappiness through your various newspapers, your various radio and television. Unfortunately I see that you support my attackers, you are accomplices declared. That is, the least we can say, very unfair, sad and bewildering. It is unimaginable, unthinkable and quite unworthy of you. You insult me, you defame me and you rejoice at my misfortune. Your attitude reflects hatred, jealousy, anger, malice, injustice, arbitrariness etc.. You are not looking for truth or knowledge saving that I teach everywhere. You do not recognize the good I do to humans, nor the countless valuable services that I can provide people with my practice and féminologique philothérapique. Instead of regret, to complain, and defend myself to sympathize with my pain and my pain, you may, instead of getting dirty, fight me, accusing me falsely and unjustly of being a terrorist, associate of bin Laden, the Communist, Socialist, Marxist-Leninist, robber, dangerous for America. You mock me, ridicule me you and you deliver me up to public condemnation. That is, to say the least, ungrateful, scandalous, diabolical, demonic and satanic. Stop making such propaganda. Stop making my contrepublicité. I do not deserve it. I, Citizen of Boston, I, the Martin Luther King a, me, the second savior of black America, I do not deserve such a fate. You are very wrong. There is nothing worse in this world transform a malefactor benefactor, a savior of mankind into a criminal. You are doing exactly the opposite of your professional duty, moral and social. I understand that you do not exist to hurt the honest people, inspired by God to help build a new world, which will be more beautiful, fairer, happier, more harmonious, more free and peaceful, a new company, beaming that will be based on truth and justice. Like me, you must work for peace, happiness, harmony and salvation of Americans and humanity. Your code of ethics forbids you to make or defend evil. Greetings, I thank and congratulate those of you who are honest, serious, wise, true and correct. They did not seek to harm me. They may know that harming me, they hurt themselves, to America and the world. As for the other, I ask them to regroup, to edit, change their negative mindset, toxic. It is never too late to do well. I forgive them their trespasses, and all their trespasses against me. I do not grudge their care. This is contrary to my nature and to the letter and spirit of my teachings philothérapiques all you need to know now. I put those who overwhelmed me with abuse, those who rejoice at my misfortune and those who do not on an equal footing. For me, friends and enemies alike. They are the same for those who live in the consciousness of God, Krishna, Buddha, Tao, Li and the laws of philothérapie. Do not be afraid of me. Do not fear me. I'm tolerant, forgiving, altruistic and compassionate toward others. This is what I teach to Americans. I know forgiveness and love. I am grateful to my benefactors as to my criminal. My conspiracy to me are more useful because they help me raise morally and spiritually. They are like my teachers and my trainers, who give me exercises to do to train and strengthen me. They work for my good, my success, my happiness and my salvation (unknowingly), things I wish for everyone. I pause here to allow you to ask me any questions you might ask me. Thank you."

Toissin saw at once nervous and excited a hand in the air, pointed at him, who wished to speak: "I am Mr. Smith, a journalist" American" Truth and Justice. My question is: What is the government of the United States of America has criticized you at your conference in the Capitol and what do you answer it today, after a while back and reflection? "Toissin had not spoken since her attack on Capitol Hill. And the press conference gave him the opportunity to comment on desired his aggression for the first time: "I owe it to truth to say that the U.S. government charged me nothing. Officially, no one told me anything. But unofficially, I was criticized for saying openly in public things unpleasant, annoying, unpleasant, that dishonor America. I was criticized for having tarnished the image of America, criticized and condemned U.S. foreign policy that is based on lethal violence, domination and exploitation of other States on military force or war. I was accused of having denounced and condemned U.S. imperialism.

But this is a misunderstanding, a bad interpretation of my speech. This is a bad comment and a quarrel that I did. In truth, I do not accuse the foreign policy of America and I do not condemn anything. My job and my duty is not to do that. My only duty is to advise American leaders what they must do to make their people happier, more prosperous, more humane, moral and spiritual. My duty is to tell them how to make their countrymen are at peace, safe, free, quiet and saved in America and abroad. I'm not in the political field but on the moral, spiritual, psychological and metaphysical. I am a caregiver. To heal and to save my patients, I have to properly diagnose them without kindness, without weakness, without fear, without cowardice, without shyness, without hypocrisy, without lies, without error or illusion. These are the conditions of my effectiveness and my professional competence. That's how I work. In all other countries of the world where I will, I will do the same thing I do here in America. Philothérapeute my work is to show politicians, businessmen and ordinary men found everywhere on earth, how to think, act and feel to succeed, find the right health, welfare, happiness and salvation. It is this work scientific, philosophical, technical and therapeutic I did on July 4th at the Capitol. If I am misunderstood, hated, challenged, fought, persecuted and punished because of it, unfortunately. Pity. So I bear my cross as Jesus Christ has done before me, among the Jews. History and God alone are the true impartial judges of everyone. They will say later if I do good or evil. If I deserve to be persecuted and killed or not. Which, for now, is certain is that I suffered here the fate of Jesus, Socrates, Thomas More, Mahatma Gandhi, Martin Luter King, Seneca, Confucius, Cicero, Malcom X, Nelson Mandela and Steve Biko, among other martyrs.

I urge you journalists to tell the truth and nothing but the truth about the nature, objectives, methodology and results of philothérapie to Americans and all humanity. This is very important. It is in good health, happiness, prosperity and salvation of mankind. It is in harmony and peace in nature, in society and in the universe. I urge you to fully understand all the benefits, value, validity, and the reason for the exceptional merit of philothérapie and féminologie. You and I are thinkers. We share the same destiny and play the same role in society.

We all informants, trainers, educators and moralists of the human race. Work together, hand in hand, as a humanist colleagues the benefit of humanity. With that, I would like to end this press conference. Thank you for your kind attention."

Since the conference held July 4 at the Capitol, Toissin lost his freedom of movement in America. He lost the right to move anywhere without encountering many difficulties, without being miles harassment of any kind, without being strictly controlled and monitored. Indeed, he was unjustly treated group Alqaïda terrorists who attacked America. And his name figured prominently on the black list of those to be hunted, trapped and arrested all because of espionage and terrorism. Many presumptions and suspicions against him. At each station and each airport, getting off a bus, a metro (train) a taxi, he was each time quickly and brutally surrounded by a horde of police officers who searched him thoroughly, thoroughly, and which threatened him. He made this dangerous experience, Boston, Chicago, Dallas, Florida, New York, Washington DC, Anderson, Cincinnati, to Tolido, Albany, Pittsburg, San Francisco, Los Angeles, Vermont, in Akron… Nevertheless, Toissin had his morale high. He was unflappable, always calm, confident and optimistic. He believed firmly in a bright future. He believed in a better tomorrow, and peaceful paradise for him and for America. He considered himself a martyr for the radiation of America. He always said work to purify the soul and the will of America and make them shine more.

After the publication of five successive sections of the newspaper very complimentary" Truth and Justice" which made an accurate account of the press conference of Empire State Building, Toissin bounces psychologically and saw his popularity soar to the last degree. Every newspaper, every radio and television all U.S. undertook to rehabilitate the CB and do it justice. They said now the truth about him. They offering incense, and were whitened the free advertising. The entire American press did nothing more than singing the praises of Toissin and lay bare its merits. For six months, the commercial product Toissin was the most popular and well sold domestically Chinindien the President through the action of the media and lobbying professional journalists. Opinion leaders turned the situation completely in favor of Toissin. They sat up all wrongs. The star's spiritual CB shone again and stronger than before. She lit up very strongly the land of Uncle Sam who finally gave up all its negative and destructive emotions: anger, hatred, jealousy, resentment, fear, contempt, pride, vanity, power complex, development, wealth of industrialization. America became reconciled with his new black savior, with Martin Luther King a. In the aftermath, the National Association of Press American (ANPA) organized a big celebration in honor of the new hero on the occasion of July 4 July 4 that followed unhappy. This was the time to educate and mobilize the entire U.S. population to express its gratitude and to pay a solemn tribute to Toissin, the martyr. So on this occasion pathetic, every American was invited and obliged to go Toissin offer a pair of glasses that would replace both symbolically blinded to CB. The ANPA offered, for its part, a cutting Toissin. The federal government distinguished by decorating the CB. Then he offered ten pilots with ten planes to help move all over the world. These ten aircraft replaced somehow broken his ten toes on Capitol Hill. The National Association of American Women (Anwa) made him a gift of ten cars representing his ten toes destroyed. Haward offered him ten with ten bus drivers. The Association of Former U.S. Presidents (FAPA) offered him a sum of ten billion. The National Association of American Medical offered him a house in Boston. This was costed at ten billion dollars. The National Association of Scholars and Philosophers Americans (ANAPS) made him a gift of a university bearing his name. The National Association of Representatives and U.S. Senators (anarchists) offered him a large golden table as Award for Excellence in Humanism. The National Association of Manufacturers Americans (ANAI) awarded him an Award for Excellence in Humanism in the amount of ten billion dollars. One month after this, Alfred Nobel came miraculously from his grave and glorious crown Toissin came in person with the Nobel Prize for Peace. This consecration Universal opened all the doors at CB. Now, it was celebrated annually and worshiped everywhere. Several monuments and headstones were erected in every city in America to glorify and immortalize. The National Association of Americans Cosmonauts

(ANAC) offered, for its part, a free trip to the moon to Toissin. She decided to install the CB there forever if he wanted. Toissin but rather preferred a simple tourist trip of short duration. So he spent three months. Only. All America prayed fervently for him and blessed his trip to the moon. We asked God to watch over him and bring him safely to earth. The National Association of Religious Americans (ANAR) dedicated to him a special mass for the great support in this pleasure trip, however, which seemed frightening to many Americans.

CHAPTER 14

CHANGE

On his return from the moon, Toissin found the fullness of his health. He enjoyed an exceptional physical health. His eyes gouged out were replaced by a multitude of moon-shaped eyes and dazzling. Now, no human could look at him and, even less secure in their eyes. His ten toes crushed by ruthless batons were replaced by an unlimited number of new and amazing toes. These were made with proper means to the inhabitants of the Moon. Ears, nose, hands, gender and language were redone, reinforced, infinitely multiplied to give him extraordinary power and unlimited. Toissin returned from the moon with a very strong message to everyone on Earth. This message was read to the lunar top of the monument, the tallest building in Washington DC, next to the White House. Reading this post was made a solemn July 4, at 1600 GMT. Any official America found itself at the Monument to hear the special message lunar. "Ladies and gentlemen, I greet you fraternally and sincerely thank you for coming so many to hear the message that the kind people of the Moon has asked me to send to you in the name of love and the friendship between the Moon and Earth. Know that I am now your Ambassador Plenipotentiary to the Moon. Upon submitting a very long list of your complaints to the state moon, here's what you said, in reply: "Inhabitants of the Earth, we, the Lunistes, perfectly know your problems, all your sufferings, all your problems and all your troubles. We charge Biongon (initiatory name given by Toissin Authorities of the Moon) that you sent us here to express our desire to help you live a happy, peaceful, healthy and in harmony with the cosmos. To do this, you should destroy all your weapons and war machines, to withdraw all your troops military stationed here and there over all the earth, close all your bases warriors who are outside your home to unscrupulous soldiers who massacred at will and with impunity other peoples. We condemn and strictly forbid all evil and political enslavement and colonization in the world. With your aggressive and barbaric behavior, you disturb the universal order and harmony, you cause disasters and crises all- out against yourselves. You receive a boomerang effect as a reward or a fair return for the harm you do in the world. You commit suicide without knowing it. We strongly urge you to abandon the destructive violence, wickedness and all the bad habits that you practice against other peoples and turning against yourself in many ways. Do you love one another and be reconciled with your enemies. Make peace with the earth and now live in happiness pure, without illusion. Get out of your ignorance known and purify your mind. Get rid of any poisonous or mental virus. Follow these tips to the letter and all will be well and good for you. Imitate our lunar civilization. It will save you. Give yours. It contains too many poisons. We, the Lunistes, are so simple, natural, happy and at peace, at home, you earthlings think, wrongly, that we do not exist. Our infinite wisdom makes us humble, modest, simple and invisible to you Earthlings. You are our opposites. You are insane, barbaric, violent, destructive, greedy, robbers material goods and wealth from everywhere, criminal, immoral, racist, slave, aggressive, colonialist, imperialist" and" occidentalocentristes. Since you earthlings have found our planet, moon, and you have planted your flag proud, vain, arrogant and belligerent, have you seen from your eyes, only one person on the moon? (No. Can you describe the inhabitants of the moon? Can you say, for example, what is the color of their skin, what is race, how big they are, what are their forms? Do you know what is the shape of their head, their nose, their ears? No. Do you know what color their hair? No. We are very discreet, prudent, good, pure, omnipotent, omniscient and omnipresent. We have the gift of ubiquity. That means we have the power to be everywhere at once, to be with us on our planet, the Moon, and Earth, the sun, Mars, Venus, Jupiter and so on. We are with you on earth, we see you but you, earthlings, you are unable to see us. We have many secrets to give you. We are humble, "nothing," "nothing" and by these means, we fill all empty spaces and all. So we control the world and the universe.

If you have something instead of nothing, or nothing, you can not go anywhere and be everywhere at once. So you, Earthlings, you can not be everywhere because you are raring to go. Your eyes see nothing. And you remain perpetually ignorant. So you say stubbornly, all ego, foolishly and dogmatically that there is no creature on the moon, the moon is not yet inhabited by human beings. This is false. Absolutely False. Change your mindset to be able to save you, yourself, and save your planet. If you destroy the earth with your innumerable vices, you will destroy yourself as (the law of cause and effect). As long as you do not change your mindset toxic and destructive, you can not come and stay with us legally and officially. And if you try, despite this warning, to come with your vices, your ugliness, your dirt and your land barbarities, we repousserons and will fight to death. Discipline your mind, remove all your vices and Sober you. Be as specific (or more than) the one you sent us. Biongon imitate and follow his advice and wise teachings. Learn how to Biongonisme through philothérapie féminologie and who are our works. Your salvation, your happiness, your health and success depend on it. Attention to the mechanization and industrialization of outrageous life! Attention to the development of science and technology and wild exaggeration of the world. This is very dangerous. This poses health and environmental problems insoluble: global warming, destruction of the ozone layer, flood, earthquakes, deforestation, desertification, water pollution, air, poisoning of humans, plants, animals, and incurable diseases so deadly. Abandon barbarocratie"" (by the reign of barbarism), the cynocratie"" (the reign rof the cynicism), the mythocratie"" (the reign of the lie), the" kleptocracy" (the rule by theft), the bellocratie"" (the reign of war) and liberal democracy which serves as a pretext and ideological foundations of modernity, secularism and all forms of perverse powers, to imperialism and occidentalocentrisme.

That, dear earthlings, the better philosophy, better science, better morals, better psychology and religion better than you should. A word, hello! ".

The message was well received lunar. Toissin was a long standing ovation by a crowd excited and surprised. It embarked on speculation and all kinds of reflections asking philosophical questions: "Now therefore the moon is a country inhabited by supermen, superior people, best, gods and sages that we Earthlings do not see with our human eyes very small and too weak? But how are they? And who made them so? Why the Moon is so far from Earth? That placed it there? Its residents say they care about our fate. Why? They say that we Earthlings are not civilized, developed or happy because of our many faults and defects materialistic and capitalist. According to them, therefore, a civilized, developed and happy is he who behaves like ascetics and renouncing Hindu or Chinese type, sadhus, yogis, (sanniasî in Sanskrit), Taoists, Buddhists and Confucians," was a man who stood by Toissin.

The CB listened very carefully to the comments of each other and spoke again: "The message of Lunistes fully confirm my opinion of all the stories I'm for the world. It supports and strengthens the philothérapie. I am in tune with the inhabitants of the moon and those of all other planets. I enjoyed my stay on the moon to visit the whole universe, to educate myself more and change my nature and my anatomy. Earthlings have made me by giving me an average size. Today, I measure ten meters. Before, I weighed only 70 kg. Now I weigh 1000 Kg past, I only had two arms and two legs like humans on Earth. Today I have a multitude of arms and legs. Once I had one head, badly made and empty. Now I have a thousand heads and they are all well made and solid. Before, I had a single nose and very short. Now I have a thousand noses and they are very long. Once I had one language and it was very short. Now I have a multitude of languages and they are very long. Before, I only had two eyes and they were very weak and helpless. Today I have an unlimited number of eyes with the power of the Moon. Formerly, I was black. Black only. Now I am both black, white, yellow and red. I no longer belong to a race. I know now that there are no human races. There are no Black, White, Yellow, Red. There is only one human family. There is the man himself or humanity. Nationalities are historical accidents. Ethnic characteristics and physical accidents are natural and socio-cultural. I now realize lunar and universalist. I live the experience of my rebirth in Biongon and my personal revolution in Biongon. With my personality biongonienne"," I appear both strange and foreign to everyone. I feel it in every eye around me.

In truth, I'm completely transformed. I am introduced to the greatest mysteries and greatest secrets of life and the world. I Biongon. That means that I gained the superior wisdom, power, magic and mystical powers lunar and interplanetary Gwa. My new name is Biongon Gongondonnin. It was given to me by the mystical forces of heaven, lunar, and interplanetary Gwa. This attribute is my insider. This name is an extraordinary force, mysterious and mystical that allows me to do everything on earth. This is the key or the solutions of all problems of the Earth. We gave it to me because I am the ambassador of the Earth and the missionary of heaven so I can save the Earthlings. I warn you now, I am no longer a simple ordinary man and vulgar that could arrest, torture, persecute, humiliate, ridicule, scorn, insult and confuse with any individual on Earth. Any attempt of aggression against my person is a dangerous mistake. This exposes the entire American society to incalculable dangers. Now, I am invulnerable, invincible and invisible when I want. This is not vanity or braggadocio. You know very well that I am against these defects. I tell you the truth and nothing but the truth. My name is a mantra Biongon Gongondonnin special effects amazing, wonderful and beautiful. I pronounce this name mantra when I feel in danger or when evil comes to me. I told you that I now have multiple heads, multiple eyes, nose several, including different languages dyed, more arms, more legs, I measure ten meters. Do you understand what that means? No. Not at all. This is a coded language, hermetic, esoteric. Is it only with your fi e physical senses or material, you see my new extraordinary dimensions? No. Do you fi me now physically bigger than before? No. In your eyes, do I really measures at this time, ten meters? No. Only those of you who are even slightly mystical things insiders can understand what I mean esoteric language. Alone may have their eyes open and exercised to see my nature, my metaphysical and invisible qualities.

Before my trip to the moon, Americans had filled me donations and gifts in kind and cash. On this day, I'll offer my turn, all those present material and financial resources to the poor, destitute, sick, homeless and needy of the earth. All physical assets will be sold and the money raised will be distributed to everyone on Earth who need to live in dignity, in peace, safe, happy. I will commit bailiffs, lawyers, sociologists and economists from around the world to make me this humanitarian work correctly and quickly.

CHAPTER 15

Just after reading the message of a political, moral and spiritual sent to the Americans by the authorities of the Moon, all newspapers, all television and radio stations all U.S. began a major campaign of public awareness and opinion U.S. to revolutionary ideas and the warning of the Moon. Journalists drove people to lobby the federal government to appliquât program of rebirth, happiness and salvation Popular designed by the Moon. The national press and public opinion were devoted to the cause of thought, ethics and discipline sent by the Moon. And all unions, all faiths, all associations and all political parties called all Americans to multiple events, to patriotic marches, civil disobedience unlimited nationwide. It instituted a climate of extreme tension, violence and unrelenting pandemonium in every city. The havoc was installed. The federal government was shaken. What confusion! What a commotion! What a mess! America was in a deadly impasse that required Aggressive action. And a fierce repression that looks like a civil war demonstrators descended on hardened leaving millions dead and untold numbers of serious injuries after one week. America was in turmoil and serious in the first revolution in history. The demonstrators demanded the immediate resignation of the government and President Chinindien. Before the hardening of the movement and extent of the damage caused serious concern, MPs, senators and most ministers took to the streets. They joined the protesters very determined to bring down the bourgeois, materialistic, secular, capitalist and bellicose infernal Chinindien. This unexpected support politicians galvanisèrent revolutionary insurgents of all stripes. After three weeks on national television, which had ceased to issue two weeks ago, announced in a special edition of ten minutes and, to everyone's surprise, the government in its entirety, the National Assembly and the Senate were dissolved and the President gave his resignation Chinindien. It announced the immediate formation of a National Committee of Hi and Public Happiness (CNSBP) which was to be responsible to liquidate the current business and create the Commonwealth of Independent States and Sovereigns (CEIS). Television added, to everyone's amazement, the president of CNSBP was Toissin, CBWhile all of America fell into a trance. Explosions of joy here, weeping and wailing there. America was plunged into total confusion in which everyone spoke in his own way, his humor, his mood, his thoughts and feelings. Overall, the policy decisions announced were well received. Most U.S. citizens were jubilant and went into raptures. According to an official survey, 95% of Americans favored the revolutionary change that brought the Citizen of Boston (CB) to head the new U.S. State miniaturized. The CNSBP quickly gave himself a Prime Minister, of Indian race, and created ministerial positions in very small numbers: Worship Ministry, Ministry of Citizenship, Ministry of Public Health, Ministry of public morality, wisdom Department of Public Ministry civil peace and social ministry of public liberty, Department of public welfare, Ministry of Justice, Ministry of Public hello, Ministry of public charity, ministry of compassion, altruism Department, Ministry of Love the next, Ministry of Human Nature, Ministry of National Solidarity, Ministry of universal harmony, Department of Public Welfare, Ministry of life.

This special government, revolutionary, had to work to change the minds poisoned and toxic of all Americans. Its main task was to ensure that there is no war in the world and that America is reconciled to itself and with the rest of the world. Ministries of defense and public safety are removed, America had more soldiers, warriors to wage war in America, Europe, Africa, Asia and Oceania. It was a radical change, a great novelty, a spiritual and moral revolution. America was now working for peace. Just for peace. Through the love of neighbor and of God, justice, charity, compassion, wisdom and renunciation of life purely socio-material, the main source of all evil, of all conflicts, all the violence and of war. All factors or means of warfare should be destroyed. Rapidly destroyed. The heavy and light weapons, sophisticated, terrifying of mass destruction (nuclear weapons, the atomic bomb) were destroyed in a month. Agreements of peace, happiness, salvation and mutual health were signed with all African, Arab and Asian countries that once were safe and deadly enemies of America: Afghanistan, Iraq, Pakistan, Iran, Korea north, Somalia, Libya, Vietnam now... The war left the place at the bilateral, multilateral, appeased for the prosperity and development of love, compassion, altruism, philanthropy, empathy, solidarity, justice, charity.

President Toissin wanted to make America the crossroads of heaven and earth. For that, America was renamed Divine Paradise on Earth (PDT). In this place, all the vices and sins of the past were removed: exploitation of man by man, oppression, crime, delinquency, crime, misery, poverty, evil, injustice, arbitrariness, tyranny bourgeois competition murderous savagery, cruelty, violence, negative, pederasty, lesbianism, prostitution, drug abuse, suffering, misfortune, fatal diseases, materialism, individualism, egotism, selfishness, pride, vanity, fear, stress, anxiety... All poisons and all viruses were systematically and mental totally destroyed in a month. Construction of Divine Paradise knew Earth was accelerated. Very fast. Toissin dreamed of creating the Union of Earth and Moon (UTL) as the first phase of its global political, humanitarian, moral and spiritual: the creation of the Universal Nation (UN) which will be directed and governed by the inhabitants of the Moon. He received these missions during his trip memorable and historic on the Moon. He had to accomplish this promptly on pain of being punished and replaced by someone else. The CB was eager and proud to make these grandiose plans to satisfy his masters and sponsors spiritual and cosmic. He had no time to eat or sleep. His duties were enormous and overwhelming. The ignorance of the vulgar Earthlings grew to doubt him and his ability to carry out all these glorious works. People treated him with arrogant, pretentious megalomaniac delusional and insane.

The United States of America (USA) disappeared as the Union of Socialist Republics, Soviet (USSR) Lenin. Its nostalgic formed several bands of thugs, thieves and terrorists to fight this change they disliked.

Of anti-Ku Klux Klan Toissin were created. They prowled day and night around the presidential palace. Their mission was to kill the C.B.. And multiplied these formidable terrorist attacks against the murderous members of the revolutionary government. More than once, was arrested Toissin, surrounded, shot, shot, bombed and left for dead. But Toissin is Toissin. He remained equal to itself. Biongon was prepared to resist at all hazards. His supernatural powers and on-land still save him. Front of every danger, every attack, he recited his mantra, his mantra, magic, that made him instantly invisible, invulnerable and invincible" Bion-gon-gon-gon-gift-nin." It instantly took it out of danger by transporting miraculously to the Moon or Domolon. To return to Earth or in America, he had to recite the same mantra in reverse:" nin-don- gon-gon-gon-bion." Thus he long resisted his incorrigible enemies and escape to countless attacks and coups.

Despite numerous difficulties and challenges in all directions, the CNSBP worked tirelessly, fiercely and absolute conviction. And after seven months already, he managed to eliminate many of ills in the country. Even if sometimes met fierce opposition on the most sensitive issues, from the nostalgic, the mafia, dark forces, reactionary, anti-revolutionary, conservative and reactive. The revolution triumphed imposed by the Moon. After a year, began to fall off. They were beautiful and very sweet. Thus the difficult problem of prostitution was solved. Across the country, we could not see a single prostitute or a single prostitute. How it could it be? By changing the mindset of the prostitutes come from the teachings of the Moon which were broadcast in an extraordinary way across the country. By finding work at all prostitutes. This allowed them to live decently and with dignity. They also found husbands and wives.

The problem of homosexuality and pedophilia was solved by the moralizing and excessive spiritualization of Americans also came from the moon. The problem of drug abuse, addiction, was solved by the same method. The problem of armed robbery, gang activity, burglary, robbery and banditry was solved in the same way. The problem of economic and financial crisis, recession, unemployment, misery, poverty, exploitation of workers resolved by the abolition of the capitalist and liberal system and the adoption of the socio-economic Moon. This new system ignores the currency, industrialization, speculation mafia, conspicuous consumption, pillage, waste and depletion of natural resources, energy, property and natural resources, the exploitation of man by man. It is based on the return to nature and frugality. In this system, the golden rule taught to all, which gave the well-being, health, happiness and salvation was poverty. Yes, poverty, term diverted from its true meaning noble and salutary, which means balance and harmony. Poverty and wealth, two things extreme, opposing poverty. They are harmful. The political problem solution found in the lunar imitation of the political system. This was based on self-excluding any violence and negative stress. This system was neither monarchy nor republic. It was all that and none of it. It included all political systems, past, present and future. He was dynamic and harmonious synthesis of all models of society and power. He was the dialectical transcendence of all political ideologies land: liberalism, communism, socialism, communalism, communitarianism, nationalism, etc. theocracy. It was dominated by the philosophy and ethics of ascetic renunciation. All Americans had become ascetics. They left their moral selfish, barbaric and materialistic-based competition and the scramble for money, material wealth with evil, wickedness, injustice, cruelty and crime. All became Buddhists, yogis, Hindoos, Taoist, Confucian, bossonistes"""" biongonistes, paysanocrates"""" and" afrocrates lunaristes." Life became bearable now, easy, virtuous, beautiful and happy. America was well saved by the lunar civilization and culture based on peace and general official practice of the virtues of love, compassion, altruism, empathy, solidarity and charity.

After ten years, gradually, Toissin built a beautiful new American nation following the lunar model. For the inhabitants of the moon, the new America Toissin (PDT) was simply the capital of the new nation that would emerge from the merger of all the nations of the earth and moon (UTL).

"Ladies and Messiers, dear compatriots, my mission on earth is finished. Universal Nation (N.U.) exists. All your dreams have become realities. The sacrifices made to achieve these glorious results are extensive and significant. Many of us have lost their lives, their souls in Peace! Those have now entered the national and world history. Glory to them. We, the survivors will never forget them. Universal Nation to which they gave their blood and their lives is very grateful. It annually celebrate their memory. She will dedicate their several monuments to perpetuate their memory in the collective memory. I give, on this solemn day, glorious, my resignation. I leave my position as President and founder of CNSBP and guide and inspirer of the revolution and special saving. From that day, I joined the Authorities of the Moon that I eagerly await for me given a new mission. Thank you to you all. Farewell! Bion-gon-gon-gon-gift-nin! ". Toissin, CB, disappeared immediately after this speech touching and memorable recounted the long history of tragic-drama of the American Revolution and the moon. Now the name Toissin (gwa hero language of Côte d'Ivoire) had become a great universal symbol. It was celebrated annually around. Especially Domolon, Ivory Coast, in the Sub-Prefecture Alépé (near Abidjan) where Toissin was born and where he was early initiated into the secrets and mysteries of the gods and geniuses Biongon Gongondonnin of Gwa people (or M'Batto) before leaving for America. The magical power of Gwa, valiant warriors fearless, invincible, invulnerable and invisible to much, is due to their ancestors, two supernatural beings and surterrestres, who protect and assist them forever and wherever they are. The story of the magical power of Gwa is verifiable and verified Domolon currently. It's true cultural history of a people. The founding story, invigorating and fortifying the people Gwa.

The greatness and glory of Toissin are due to his work and his exceptional genius. Indeed, he alone, as the special product of Domolon, America and the Moon, was able to solve all the difficult political, economic, social, cultural, spiritual, moral and axiological Earth. He ended the barbarocratie"" (by the reign of barbarism), to autocracy (individual or personal power, authoritarian), the mythocratie"" (the reign of the lie), the " kleptocracy" (the reign of the flight), the cynocratie"" (the reign by the vulgar cynicism), the bellocratie"" (the reign of war), the ethnocracy" (management of state power by and for one ethnic group who plundered all the property and wealth of the country by despising and crushing all other ethnic groups). All these forms of perverse and dangerous to be practiced especially in black Africa, the continent's original Toissin. They cause repeated coups, civil wars, genocide and armed rebellions. Behind these massacres, are the former European colonizers who support regimes that are favorable and profitable, the puppet regimes and corruptible to wish to pay and total devotion to the Western imperialists. In this dynamic, Western countries behave in slavery, as racist, colonialist and neo-colonialists in unrepentant. These are states aggressors, invaders, bandits and thugs (AXIS OF EVIL). These are the states wild, mafia, negative and toxic. They are ruthless conquerors states that use three kinds of ways to establish their total domination of the world and achieve their political, economic and cultural rights: their military forces, their Judeo-Christian religion, languages and schools or education systems. Their weapons are intended to wars of occupation and exploitation of weaker states. Their religion is intended to lull the minds with lies infantilizing, and to facilitate the submission and exploitation of their colonies. Schools require all cunningly and artfully values of their civilization colonized and alienated culturally indoctrinate them.

BY THE SAME AUTHOR

The Golden Rules of Personal Success, Happiness, Health and Salvation, unpublished manual of philotherapy.
Introduction to Philotherapy, unpublished essay
The Conditions of Woman Happiness, philotherapy essay, Afro-Star editions, 2011
Introduction to Oriental Philosophy, essay, Afro-Star editions, 2011
Oriental Philosophy Anthology, essay, Afro-Star editions, 2010
State Lies, unpublished novel
The Nastiness of the President, unpublished stories
African Revolution, unpublished plays
Apartheid,Stop! unpublished plays
What Future for Ivorians and Africans, unpublished essay
The Solution of Ivorians and Africans Political Problems, unpublished essay
Electoral Code, novel, Black Stars Editions, 1995
Côte d'Ivoire is Forbidden, novel, Black Stars Editions, 1992
Portrait of Good and Bad Voter, of Good and Bad Candidate, essay, Black Star Editions, 2000
The Eleven Evils of Côte d'Ivoire, essay, Afro-Star Editions 2005
Côte d'Ivoire with its Foreigners, essay, Black Stars Editions, 2002
The Guidebook of African Philosophy, Black Stars Editions, 1985
The Political Thought to Rescue Côte d'Ivoire, essay, Black Stars Editions, 2003
Afrocratism, unpublished essay
Ahikaba, novel, 2012.